# About the Author

Luise Noring is a Danish citizen who has spent more than fifteen years living in different countries across the world, broadening her understanding of people, cultures and languages. When asked why she has spent so many years living and traveling abroad, Noring answers, "Curiosity." In fact, curiosity best captures her pursuit of knowledge that has guided her entire life. In her previous careers, Noring was an academic scholar of economics and ran her own international consultancy company. The book draws on in-depth research knowledge and practical experience with the people, countries and cultures of the world.

For further information, please visit: www.luisenoring.net

# Going Places, Somewhere and Nowhere

**Luise Noring**

# Going Places, Somewhere and Nowhere

Olympia Publishers
*London*

**www.olympiapublishers.com**
OLYMPIA PAPERBACK EDITION



A CIP catalogue record for this title is
available from the British Library.

ISBN: 978-1-80439-361-1

This is a work of fiction.
Names, characters, places and incidents originate from the writer's
imagination. Any resemblance to actual persons, living or dead, is
purely coincidental.

First Published in 2023

Olympia Publishers
Tallis House
2 Tallis Street
London
EC4Y 0AB

Printed in Great Britain

# Prologue

Europe and North America were where the war had started. Some would say Europe and North America were the aggressors. The war started between Russia and "old" Europe but soon enlisted the U.S. Once the U.S. was officially part of the war, groups from South America that sympathized with Russia attacked the U.S. from the south.

Only a year into the war, Europe and North America were a flaming sea of intense horror and complete carnage. It seemed that the whole world was fighting Europe and North America on their own territories, destroying everything in its wake. Especially the large cities were completely wiped out.

Out of this destruction, new societies emerged, centered on the old metropolises. These societies did not evolve within the nation state. The global map was dissolved. The new societies adhere to the declared factions organized around online communities. The declared factions are entirely global from their inception. The nation state becomes a thing of the past.

At the end of five years of intense fighting, people lose sight of who is the ally and who is the enemy. Nobody seems to remember what caused the war and who started it. The faction warnings released to the online communities decide who fights against whom. If a group of strangers approach and the warning sounds, people get ready for combat. In this way, the algorithm of each declared faction proscribes who is the ally and who is the enemy. Nobody understands the algorithms. Ergo nobody understands the war.

Eventually, war calms down in Europe and North America. It leaves behind a desert of destruction. As declared factions grow stronger and larger, they expand through continued fighting that moves from Europe to Africa and from North America to South America. Africa and South America are now fighting for their lives. In this way, the war becomes an unstoppable monstrous animal of destruction that moves across the world, incenting war everywhere it goes. The animal's brain is the different algorithms warring within it. Humans created those algorithms. Humans have since lost control of them.

# The War



*One year earlier*
*Copenhagen, Denmark*

"It is just a parenthesis," she says. It sounds comforting and makes the disarray of chaos seem easy to overcome. But that is not actually what she is feeling. She feels she is in the middle of chaos. Everywhere she looks, there is upheaval, and most worrying, there is nothing to replace it with. Just chaos, upheaval and emptiness. It does not feel like a parenthesis, but maybe if she can convince herself that it is just a parenthesis in a long-lived life, she is able to get through it. The same kind of thinking helped her in the past.

She is quiet, thinking and taking in the thought. That is how she is. When she does not know what to say, she doesn't say anything. She does not try to fill the empty void with empty words. Instead, she reflects in silence on what is being said. For some people, the quietness is interpreted as reclusion and remoteness. Like an arrogance that she does not possess. She just feels like thinking. She can, or so she believes, think herself out of any problem. Except she cannot think herself out of this one. Every time she thinks she has a solution, something to hold on to, that solution too unravels.

"Maybe the universe is trying to tell you something," she says. "Maybe it is trying to say something first by tickling you with a feather in the ear. You wave it away. Then it comes back with a gentle push. You push back. Then it comes back and back till you have nothing left and must reset the course of your life.”

“WHAT THE FUCK DO YOU WANT, UNIVERSE! Go fuck up someone else’s life! Why me? Leave me alone,” she is screaming inside.

“What if all people’s lives are this difficult?” she thinks. “Perhaps we just don’t know about it because everybody walks around carrying their own problems in silence.” This is why the older we get the more our bodies collapse under the weight of problems. Young people have a bounce in their steps. They can conquer the world. The older you get, the more you realize that you are in a constant battle with the universe to be left alone to live the life you want. “LEAVE ME ALONE!” No, the universe does not want to leave her alone. She has somehow called the universe’s attention to her existence, and now it is causing havoc in her life.

She always has a plan. She needs a plan because it gives her the sense of control. Her life can be planned. Now her life is a blank page. No, it is a hurricane. She trying to use the temporary calm at the eye of the storm to think through every solution, only to see each solution carried away by the hurricane. Little by little, she loses a bit more. Like peeling the layers of an onion. One by one. Until you get to the core. To the essence.

She has nothing left. No job. No home. Her twin girls are leaving for school. Her long-term love that she thought she should grow old with. The pandemic has left deep marks on her life. The pandemic is the culmination of decades of global tension. Countries are closing inwards. Hostility is growing between them.

Deterioration of livelihoods in the physical world encourages people to rally around a culpable enemy in the cyber world. Feeds and online communities offer a parallel, more appealing world of likeminded followers. At the same time, there are global movements drawing the world to war. As the world becomes more globalized, it becomes evident how countries, cities and communities differ. Across the world, people access and enroll in global online communities of the likeminded. Divisions emerge within countries, cities and communities, and grow and expand beyond countries, cities and communities. It is a global clash of ideologies.

The factions became almost like religions. They have their own belief systems they swear by, and they show no mercy to people of other beliefs.

War is looming, penetrating the air with deep hatred. The tension between us and them is thickening. No one can see the polarization nor the approaching war with their naked eye. Yet, everyone feels it like a staunch chill in their bones. It is just a matter of time before the tension erupts.

The reality of war is becoming more and more stark. She realizes that her problems will disappear in this new global context. She realizes that her problems are dwarfed by the scale of the global problems that are now unfolding. A third world war will replace everybody's daily struggles with the gigantic struggle of survival.


*Today*
*Northern part of Denmark*


Two factions, each consisting of hundreds of thousands of people, pass each other deep in the forest in total silence. Only the rattling of dry leaves makes noise. No one dares to speak a word. If one word is spoken, direct combat erupts. No one dares to tempt destiny. A defensive move is easily interpreted as an aggressive move. The situation can easily escalate into battle and eventually a long-stretched war, where both parties continuously retaliate.

She realizes that she often found herself in the forest when she is looking for herself. Her deep relationship with the forest started when she was a child. She took refuge in the forest when her father lost his temper at her at night. It was about deeply rooted mental illness. Maybe it was because her father was a homosexual trapped in a relationship with a woman. A woman that during her childhood had an amazing career trajectory that culminated with her becoming the highest paid CEO in Denmark. Her father was educated, a fashion designer from Saint Martin's in London. He had started a promising career in Switzerland, only to come back to Copenhagen when his mother took ill.

The bond between mother and son was strong and full of conflicts and contradictions. In Denmark, he had had a design career of considerable standing, but with time, his fashion career evaporated. Instead, he moved into real estate, spending his wife's hard-earned money on purchasing real estate. Eventually, these monies evaporated, too, during the crash in the early 1990s, leaving her mother to die penniless in social housing.

Her mother is her shining star. She had died five years ago, but she still thought of her mother every day. She still bemoaned the loss of her mother every day. Her mother was a brilliant woman. She was intelligent. She raised her children as if they were real people. Not children. She asked and listened with curiosity to what they had to say. She rarely told her daughter what to do or not to do. Her mother wanted her to live her own life and make her own experiences.

During the dead of night, she slips out and wanders in the forest. The forest is reliable and dependable. People are deceitful and dangerous. During her walks at night, the forest protects her. It caresses her cheeks with a gentle, light wind. The branches reach down toward her, comforting her with love. She goes to the forest to pray.

Sleepless nights and the pressure of home life took their toll on her schooling. She could barely make it through school. Still, in ninth grade, she was unable to read with any fluidity. She lived in her own world. Her world was a safe world. A good world. Nobody could harm her in her world.

Dysfunctional families become close-knit families. Children of dysfunctional families grow up thinking that whatever they are experiencing is normal. Only in adolescence did it occur to her that maybe this was not how all families lived. She told her mother about the beatings. Some of them occurred in the light of day in the basement. The basement was a terrible place. Ironically, her parents had decided to create a big playroom in the basement.

On a monthly basis, her father would get angry. It was no fault of hers. Maybe it was because he felt humiliated by his lack of success vis-à-vis his wife. He would run up into her room and order her down the stairs. Down to the basement. Her legs were shivering. She wet her pants. She held tight to the railing with both hands, walking down the wide stairway in the main hallway, so that his abrupt shoves to her back would not make her fall down the stairs. Once, when they were at the top of basement stairs, her father lost control. As he gave her a hard shove in the back, she fell down the stairs and into the hard stone wall. She tried to collect herself. She felt ashamed and humiliated. The father humiliated her because that made him feel better about his own humiliation. It was that simple. Once, in the basement, he yelled and screamed at her. He hit her. If she wept, his beating picked up. If she peed in her pants, his beating picked up. She both wept and peed.

Telling her mother caused some commotion, but nothing that measured up with the charges made against her father. She conceived a plan. She had to get away. For several months, she did not speak a word to her father. She wanted to punish him in the only way she knew. He largely avoided confrontations with her. At the same time, she worked her mother, talking her into letting her go. Eventually, the whole situation became too much, and she had a massive nervous breakdown when she was twelve. The family doctor came. She explained what had happened under the watchful eyes of her father.

Shortly afterwards, she was allowed to leave for boarding school in Switzerland. Here she met other children as distressed and distraught as herself. Hurt children hurt. Behind the veneer of wealth, cruelty goes unnoticed. People mistakenly think that rich people "have it all." For a while, maybe, some people do have it all. But this has nothing to do with wealth.

*A year later*
*Somewhere in Germany*

She and her twin daughters, Ranger and Rocket, are free factioneers. Her daughters are not identical twins. They are very different. Ranger is the first born. She is taller. She is easy-tempered, open-hearted and pays close attention to people at the periphery. Rocket is more withdrawn and sensitive. She is a keen observer. She has a willpower that can move mountains. She has more temper. Both daughters are composed of key characteristics of their mother. However, they have refined and perfected those characteristics. The girls have a strong unbreakable bond. When they were younger, she often felt left out, as the girls' strong relationship was self-sufficient. Their absolute attention on each other isolated them from others, including their mother. It isolated them from the rest of the world.

As free factioneers, they have not declared their alliance to any one faction. The declared factions center on online communities and seek to gain land territories for their communities in the real world. As free factioneers, she and her daughters are free to roam the world. Nevertheless, they stay far away from declared faction settlements, which are growing in number and power.

The declared factions are the very fabric of war. They shape and sharpen the war. Each declared faction emerged out of an online community. Each online community is permeated by a strong ideology. Rather than a world defined by nation states and their borders, a new, messier world order emerges from the global online communities and their ideologies. The ideologies proscribe a black-and-white right and wrong. Members of the online communities sit anywhere in the world. Pockets of allies and enemies sit anywhere in the world.

Out of the war, four large declared factions rise: the Freedom Fighters, Prosperity, Liberators and the Patriots. The declared factions war to claim territory in the real world. The Freedom Fighters congregate along the Atlantic coast of the formerly known U.K., including Ireland and the British Isles. Prosperity controls mainland U.K. and the coastline toward continental Europe. Liberators and the Patriots have split between them formerly known North America. The Liberators primarily center on the Midwest and the southern U.S., while the Patriots reign along both coastlines.

The online communities are the backbone of each faction. Even the free factions have online sites and platforms, where they communicate. The satellites hosting the online communities are of critical importance. Without the satellite, no community; without an online community, no faction. War is both waged on the ground between factions and in cyberspace, targeting the satellites.

This is a messy world indeed. It consists of two parallel worlds: an online world and a physical world. The war of minds based on ideologies is waged in cyberspace. This world is reigned over by algorithms that play a more and more significant role. Algorithms have taken over control of the online communities. They have an unbreakable inertia by which they multiply in size and grow in complexity. They are the real rulers of people's minds. Algorithms have become the supreme masterminds of each declared faction both in the online and physical world. In the real, physical world, people are wandering around, seemingly aimlessly, in search of their online community. This is a messy world indeed. People are living in a real-time, real-life experiment.

During their wandering, they reach a gathering place that serves food and wine and offers a place to sleep. They are tired. She is too tired to bother reflecting on her scarcity of money to pay for their stay when her daughters excitedly jump up and down, pleading with her to get a real meal and a real bed.

Once inside, they sit down at a large wooden table flanked by two long benches. A woman comes over with the meal of the day. It is a hearty and healthy meal. The room is large, with a gallery running along the first floor to the rooms. She turns her head and closes out all the noise of the room to hear what the Asian man sitting at the table next to theirs is saying. "In Asia, the war has not taken quite such a heavy toll. Destruction is less prevalent and limited to the larger cities. People are not just wandering aimlessly around, trying to find lost ones and a peaceful place to settle."

"So, why did you come here?" a person from the crowd yells out.

"I was sent here by my family to look for my sister and her two boys." He looks down. "It is impossible. Everybody is moving around. No one is where they are supposed to be."

The Asian man's name is Atlas. He is a short man of slight figure. He looks positively youthful. At a distance, he could pass as a teenage boy, despite being well into his forties. His dress and demeanor resemble that of a teenager's. He wears loose jeans, an oversized t-shirt and a cap that he sometimes turns one hundred and eighty degrees, making him look even more youthful. She wonders if he is a bit immature. She is curious to understand him. It is no coincidence that Atlas dresses in this way. He pays great attention to his casual wear and the impression he makes on other people. His dress and demeanor potentially bely an insecurity, a need to show off, or both.

As she gets to know him, she realizes that he is portentous. He demands to be always taken seriously. His need for recognition and acknowledgment becomes tedious, while his inability to laugh at himself draws a parallel to a child's demand to be taken seriously by its parents. There is a sense of "Look at me!" rolled over into the expectation of applause. This makes Atlas' relationship to other people slightly strenuous. People do not relax in the company of the Atlas, as he seems overly sensitive to other people's perceptions of him. He is constantly holding back and keeping up the façade. Atlas tells himself that from this slightly withdrawn position, he can observe other people in a clearer light, which would be true if he possessed such skills of observation. Unfortunately, he does not possess such skills, as he is too preoccupied with other people's perceptions of him. He holds a mirror to other people, looking at his own reflection in other people rather than meeting them on neutral ground.

After a while, people redirect their attention away from Atlas. She grabs the chance to move over next to him. "Where in Asia are you from?" She leans toward him, as if they are going to have an intimate conversation.

"I am from Bali, of all places. It was paradise before the war. Today, even more so! At least compared with what I have seen so far in Europe."

"Do you have any war and fighting on the ground in Bali?" She looks up at him with an intense look, as if to verify the truth of what he is saying.

"No. Not really," he replies.

She knows that the war rages particularly violently in Europe and North America. Yet, the fighting is now spreading to elsewhere in the world. Atlas continues, "Smaller isolated islands seem to have been spared to some extent."

She bursts out, "I have a house in Bali, if it is still standing."

"It will still be standing." He looks at her with a

compassionate smile. They sit next to each other in silence. In silence, because no words can describe the horror going on around them. In silence, because they are both thinking about how to get to Bali.

Atlas was the opportunity she had been looking for, for years. "If I help you find your sister and her boys, will you help my daughters and me get back to Bali?" She is almost surprised to hear herself saying it.

He jumps in his seat. He looks at her in total shock. "Would you do that?" he says.

She confirms, "Yes! I really want to go back to Bali. It is a safe haven for us. People here are declaring themselves to the large factions and enrolling in a lifetime of monitoring and control. It is not a life I want for myself and my girls." She turns around and gestures with her hand out into the room. "This place is one of the few bastions of free factioneers." Her eyes well up. "I fear it is just a matter of time before we are all forced into a lifetime declaration to one of the large factions. It is sold to us as the only safe place on earth. They say they will protect us. But many people live like slaves in the large factions. They are not even safe from war. We are used as cannon fodder. I need to find the last bit of strength within me to get my girls to faction-free land and freedom."

Atlas nods and looks down. "The problem is, I have no idea where to find my sister. I have no idea how to get back to Bali. I am stuck in an eternal search in no man's land." He takes a deep breath. "When I first got here, I could not understand why everybody was wandering. They are not going anywhere. Now I am like them. Just wandering around, searching. It is hopeless."

*Still a year later*

19

As some of the declared factions grow stronger and larger, they start introducing systems and structures. For instance, if you are amongst one of the first ten thousand factioneers signed up for an online community, you are allowed to run as a candidate for the management committee, and you can vote for members of the management committee. The only requirement is that you have a chip incorporated in your stomach with a tracking device. The chip alerts you to the near proximity of enemies and allies.

In her other life, she lived in the Danish society and knew from own experience what the lack of privacy and the lack of owning your own data meant. She was not going to give up on her anonymity again without a fight. She recognized that if you do not own your own data, you do not own yourself. She knew that systems and structures have a compulsion to become overly complex and complicated. It requires enormous resources to maintain and safeguard systems and structures. They have a multiplier effect. Governments build a system and structure to monitor and safeguard systems and structures. And so on.

In Denmark, before the outbreak of the war, the level of digitalization and information integration was impressive. With one yellow card and a barcode, any citizen could go to any doctor, clinic and hospital, and their entire medical history and sometimes even that of their ancestors would be made available. All health services were publicly funded and available to all Danish citizens. With a social security number, social authorities and other authorities could access your entire life, including earnings, taxes, marital status, medical history, living, education, employment, crime, etcetera. Every citizen was a vessel of information. This information was readily available to the government authorities. Citizens did not own their own information. They did not own their own lives. Control and monitoring penetrated every corner of every citizen's existence. They say the Danish society was based on trust. But in fact, the piercing monitoring and persistent control of every Danish citizen evidenced that it was in fact based on mistrust, rather than trust. The mantra of Danish politicians was "Trust is good, but control is better."

One would think that with such fully integrated systems and information readily available about all citizens, the need for resources, systems and structures would be radically reduced. However, the multiplier effect of systems and structures meant that Denmark had the highest number of public sector employees in the world. The resource requirements for monitoring and controlling systems and structures were enormous. Vast amounts of predominately skilled labor were needed for monitoring and controlling the complex systems and structures put in place to monitor and control the fully integrated systems and structures. Systems and structures have a built-in inertia.

*Still a year later*
*Somewhere in Germany*

"I am part of a network. It is a free faction, where people are free to opt in and out as they please. They are not committing to a lifetime of loyalty. They work and contribute to any free faction on a voluntary basis. It is just one of a few platforms left for free factioneers. On this platform are some of the most tech-savvy and smart people. They still work for a free world." She explains to Atlas that she has an old friend from the old world. His name is the Plague. He has become a well-known hacker and protector of the free factioneers. "I have word that he lives in a deserted military compound in Oban in Scotland," she says and continues, "I am sure, if we find him, he will help us."

Atlas, her daughters and she form the traveling search party that will look for the Plague. With his help they will find Atlas' sister and her two boys. Eventually, they all will find their way back to Bali.

She had been to Oban in Scotland when she was about thirteen years old. The city sits on a cliff hanging high above the turbulent Atlantic Ocean. The waves reach up to the city. When she was last there, she looked out at the ocean and promised herself then and there to come back to capture its beauty again as an adult. Only one other time did she make such a promise to herself. It was when she woke up at the age of eight on a train going along the Nile River in Egypt. When she saw the beautiful pale-pink-and-yellow sun rise over the sand-colored pyramids, the Nile River and the fields it fed, she made that promise. She knew then, she had to witness this beauty again in her life. The promises we make to ourselves are the most important promises. We must keep them to stay true to ourselves.

*A year and four months later*
*Oban, Scotland*

The compound where the Plague lives is well hidden. They climb down toward the violent ocean, where the only entrance to the compound is located. The entrance is carved into the rock that the city of Oban sits on. It is more easily accessible from the water, but they do not have a boat. The climb down is strenuous and dangerous. One wrong step and you fall into the ocean, smashed against the rocks in the high waves. "Do not look down!" she keeps yelling, not knowing if anyone can hear it. The noise of the waves breaking against the rocks is deafening. She feels her legs trembling under her. She tries to focus and concentrate.

Further down the cliffside, they find a path offering steady ground. The noise from the ocean is still overwhelming. She looks at her girls and feels her eyes watering up. One of her daughters puts a hand on her shoulder to comfort and gently push her along the path. "We must keep moving. If we stall, we are at risk of being caught."

At the end of a ten-minute walk, they stop on a cement landing. There are small boats and a large ship rocking in the water of the entrance to the compound. They cannot enter the compound without going into the water or onto one of the boats. "We should borrow one of the boats," Atlas says and waves his hand toward a small rowboat. Her daughters reel the rowboat toward them. They all get in and carefully start to paddle through the entrance.

Once they enter the compound, the silence is as deafening as the ocean outside. She holds her breath. What if she has gotten it wrong! What if the Plague is not here? What if he does not want to help her? She thinks, "It is too late for regrets. We must hope we encounter friendly people in here."

"Turn off your phones! We do not want any warnings," Atlas suddenly yells as they enter the pitch darkness of the compound.

The air is cold to their bones. It smells of old cement. It smells of deserted industry. Suddenly, the boat is forced to a halt. A bright light blinds them. She puts her hands up above her eyes and speaks out into nothing. "We are friendly. We have come to seek help. We are free factioneers." She keeps on repeating this till someone pulls the boat toward the shore. A hand reaches out to help her off the boat, then her daughters and Atlas.

About ten people greet them. A woman called Harvest addresses her. "Who are you? And how do you know of us?" Harvest is about her age. She has gray hair and a youthful composure. She speaks fast. "You must tell us how you know about us," she insists.

She tries to compose herself before answering Harvest. She knows that one wrong word could end their lives. She is both excited and scared as she explains that she somehow managed to stay sporadically in touch with the Plague. She is hoping to see him now.

The ten people of the greeting party, Atlas, her daughters and she all walk up a flight of winding stairs. At the top of the stairs, they enter a huge, dimly lit hall. It has carpets, tables and chairs. It is a nice room. It is warm and dry. More and more people come into the room to greet them. People sit around them, silently watching them eat. They are starving. She tries to restrain herself and keep a calm demeanor. "I am looking for an old friend," she talks out into the room in a loud voice, "I think he goes by the name the Plague in this world. I am not sure. I knew him in the old world."

Harvest tilts her head. "We do not know who you are talking about. Never heard of the Plague," she says and looks out into the room.

They are shown to a large room with stacked beds. "You can sleep here." A young man points them to some beds. "You must be tired after traveling." They are exhausted. Too exhausted to even contemplate who these people are, where they come from and why they are living here. Within a few minutes, they are all fast asleep.

She wakes up the following morning with a deep-seated

feeling of unrest. This happens often in the mornings. She would be half-asleep and half-awake. She wakes up at six thirty every morning. This morning, she is in deep sleep as the alarm goes off. She was dreaming that a red liquid – either blood or red wine – had been spilled. In her dream, she watched as the red liquid spread across the floor. Her now deceased mother was also watching. Her daughter was wiping up the liquid from the floor. She felt gratitude toward her daughter for wiping up the liquid. She could only watch as the liquid spread. She was paralyzed, unable to move.

Once her mind redirects its attention away from the dream and toward the physical world, deep-seated disbelief and unrest creep into her mind. Another day of uncertainty. Another day of pointless existence. Another day of waiting. These feelings often try to inhabit her mind in the early mornings, on the edge of sleep and awake. She lies in the dark room, thinking about her life… Everything is in limbo.

She knows she can either embrace and embody the uncertainty or she can separate herself from it. Observe it at a distance. This is what she decides to do. She decides that disbelief, unrest and uncertainty are things that are occurring in her life. They are not her. They do not define her. She defines her. In this way, she is able to keep feelings of disbelief, unrest and uncertainty at bay. She is able to observe them in the sober light of distance and detachment. If she lets these feelings inhabit her, they become her. They would take over her mind and body, and she would become overwhelmed by disbelief, unrest and uncertainty. Despite keeping her feelings at bay, she can't help but feel that she is waiting for something big to happen. She is waiting in anticipation of the future.

That morning, they are invited to have breakfast in the large hall. "We told you that we do not know who the Plague is." Harvests pauses. "He is here. He has become an asset that Prosperity is looking for, and we do not think they have good intentions. Therefore, we are very protective of him. He is a good guy and very good at what he is doing." The Plague has perfected his tech skills. He is hacking to learn the whereabouts of family and friends for inhabitants of the compound. He is conducting online attacks on declared factions' platforms, spreading false and misleading news. He has honed skills highly acknowledged in this world. "We will take you to see him later today," Harvest says, "maybe this evening."

Harvest stays with them all day. She takes them to see where they grow vegetables, in a tall and narrow former missile launch pad. They are grown in a vertical hydroponic garden that stretches two kilometers up into the air. A cornucopia of greenery covers the walls. About fifty people are going up and down in ropes, tending to the vegetables. They seem at peace as they carefully nip away dry leaves and collect ripe fruits and vegetables.

"It looks quite dangerous." She turns to Harvest in awe.

"It is," Harvest replies, "but we all have to do whatever it takes to survive in this hole."

"Do you ever get daylight?" she asks.

"No. Only if we go outside, which we never do. For our own security, we must stay here and not go out. Nobody must know we live here."

She sees young children, deformed from hanging in the ropes all day every day. She turns to Harvest. "Is there no other way of employing these children?"

"We realize now the toll it takes to hang in the ropes all day. Recently, we have developed a division of labor where people rotate between jobs. But that does not help these children. It is too late for them."

"It all seems very well organized." She looks at Harvest. "I mean, for a free faction you have rules, divisions of labor and so on." Harvest does not reply. One of the tantalizing allures of the free factions is that people are free. Free to come and go. Free to voluntarily contribute or not. Her words hold a subtle critique. They imply that the compound faction is adopting declared faction principles. Morphing into a declared faction.

Despite seemingly having created Shangri-La underground, the rules of existence are brutal. People have no assets – other than the things of affection they carried on their endless wanderings prior to settling in the compound. Most people only have the clothes they are wearing. The dependence on other people in the community becomes critical to each person's survival. In this world, there is no mental illness. Only if the mentally ill can adapt and survive do they stand a chance of living. There are also no drug addicts nor any other addicts. If someone loses their mind, they are killed. Some people lose their minds, as they cannot bear the loss of loved ones, or they cannot cope with the hard, laborious life underground, tucked away from daylight. If anyone goes outside without permission, they are killed. She later learns that they use the dead bodies for medicine and food.

At the bottom of the green wall, there is a massive water tank with fish that cleanse the water recycled for growing the vegetables. Everything is recycled – even themselves.

In another expansive room, animals are grazing. They are walking along a subterranean freshwater river. "We would never survive if we did not have this river," Harvest explains. "Actually, we try to keep the livestock at a minimum, so they do not contaminate the water and do not eat all the food we grow. It is a balance that I am not sure we have reached yet."



*Still a year and four months later*
*Oban, Scotland*

Harvest takes her to see the Plague later that day. "We did not want to tell you about the Plague till we were sure he knows you." She leans toward her. "We needed him to verify your story. We are very protective of him. He is valuable to our community." As they walk down a multitude of almost pitch-black corridors and narrow stairways, Harvest says, "Just because it is dark doesn't mean that there is no light." She turns around and smiles at her while she reaches both hands to her heart. The maze of corridors and stairways of the former military compound is impressive. It dates to the Second World War. Now, the compound is used and protected by the free factioneers.

They enter the dark, expansive room. Piping and cables are hanging loosely across the ceiling. Fluorescent pipe lamps shed a scarce and depressive light. He turns around. He is tall. His nose is large. He has gained weight around the midriff. "Wow! I am so happy to see an old friend from the old world. It is a miracle. How did you find me!" the Plague says while walking across the room to her and her daughters. He leans down toward her and gives her a tight hug. Amid war, such a hug makes us human and makes life worth living. She knows the Plague from her time in France. He is from Argentina but moved with his single mother to France, where he grew up. They met in France when she lived there.

The Plague is a humorous man, who seems to be on the verge of breaking out into full laughter at any moment. He lost his mother to the war, but otherwise he has lived all his life on his own. He has never had a life companion or children. This means that the war has caused less harm to him than almost any other person in his vicinity. He only has himself to look out for, and he is quite adventurous. His life is relatively less complicated than most other's. This has granted him a lighter spirit and honed his ability to smile and laugh. He attracts people that have a positive spirit and enjoy his warmth, approachability and lightheartedness.

Twelve years earlier<br>South of France

The night she met the Plague the first time, she wore a skimpy tangerine dress with gold chains across the breast and back holding the dress in place. They met in a nightclub with large palm trees plotted around the club that was built like an amphitheater. The dancefloor was the stage. She was sitting on a puff on one of the steps overlooking the dancefloor, when he came up to her with a glass of Champagne. He kneeled in front of her to offer her the glass, which she thought was quite endearing. They danced and had a nice but controlled time. French men do not like their women to lose control. It is perceived as uncool and unchic. Something she could appreciate. She was naturally quite reserved and not very flirtatious. They exchanged numbers. The Plague texted her, "It was lovely meeting you. I hope I will see you soon again."

By the time she met the Plague, she had not had sex with her husband for two years. "At thirty-nine, I am too young to sign off on sex for the rest of my life," she reasoned with her husband. In the end, they decided that she could be with other men, as long as she kept it secret and respected the family. The family became an institution. The marriage became an arrangement.

She explained the arrangement she had with her husband to the Plague. "My husband is not interested in having sex with me," she started with hesitation in her voice. She felt ashamed that he did not want her.

The Plague raised one brow and looked her up and down. "That is hard to believe."

She replied, "Not really, if you know the reason." She paused. "He drinks. Like, really drinks. Drinking is the first thing he does in the morning and that last thing he does before going to bed. If he ever goes to bed, that is." She got sad thinking about her situation. She was stuck in the South of France. A place she didn't really like. She couldn't leave for Denmark with her girls. She needed his permission as a co-parent to take the girls out of the country. If she left without the girls, she risked losing custody of them. That was out of the question. She was the only parent the girls had that took care of them.

"I don't understand how your husband cannot be interested in making love to you," the Plague said after she explained the sex-with-no-strings-attached arrangement she was proposing to him.

"Nor do I." She smiled. "Jokes aside, he has very severe alcohol issues. I can hardly recall when I last saw him sober." He nodded in a sign of understanding. It was probably not an unfamiliar phenomenon in France, or anywhere else for that matter, to have a noncommittal affair on the side of a failed marriage. She felt it was a very mature way to deal with her marriage. Nevertheless, it made her unhappy. She wanted a loving marriage rather than seeking love outside a loveless marriage. Given the situation, she was grateful of her relationship with the Plague. She sensed he fell in love with her. They never spoke about it.

After two years of a wonderfully uncomplicated and loving relationship, the Plague said, "I have a job offer in New York." He paused and looked down. "What should I do?" He looked at her and waited for her response. Her eyes were tearing up. To avoid him seeing it, she fixed her eyes to the ground. She cleared her throat and thought for a second whether he had noticed her immediate response.

She looked up. "You should go! I don't want to stand in the way of your future when I cannot give you a future. Your future is yours. Your future is not with me."

His lower lip trembled as he said, "There will always be room for you and the girls at my place in New York." They both just sat there and looked intensely at the ground. "I had better get going now," he said and let go of her hand. For a second, she resisted, but then she let go.



*Still a year and four months later*
*Oban, Scotland*

That same evening, they host a celebratory dinner in the big hall for her, her daughters and Atlas. The room is full of crystals. Bells are ringing. Pieces of colored tissue hang from the ceiling. She turns around to Harvest and says, "We are grateful for the time we have spent here with you, but we should be moving on soon." Harvest looks away, as if she does not hear her. They both know she heard her. For a moment, there is an uncomfortable atmosphere of denial between them. "Will we not be allowed to leave?" she thinks. "Surely, they can't keep us here against our will!" She suddenly feels the urge to get away right away.

Dinner is opulent with fruits, vegetables and meat. They are asked to take a center seat at a long table. She is sitting next to the Plague. He grabs her hand under the table and raises it to kiss it. "I am so happy you are here," he whispers. Small, compact pieces of soft meat are placed in front of them. This meat is particularly precious. People clap as the plates of meat are carried into the room in progression to the high table.

Thin slices are cut by a young, pretty woman, who turns and smiles at them as she places the slices of delicate meat on their plates. "What is this, and why is everybody so excited?" She turns to the Plague. He looks down and replies, "It is human brains."

She almost chokes on the food but is blatantly aware that everybody's eyes are resting on her. "I feel sick!" she whispers. She grabs the hands of her daughters and shakes her head. They all stop eating the meat.

Later that evening, she attacks the Plague with questions. "Why do you eat human brains? Where do these brains come from? The enemy?"

He looks away in shame. "These stem from three free factioneers who left the compound without permission."

"What is the difference between this free faction and the declared one above ground?" she says, upset. Above the ground, the Freedom Fighters rule. Further inland, Prosperity rules. She does not leave him time to reply but continues while catching her breath. "There is NO difference! How will we get away from here? I will not live and die here. My daughters will not live and die here!"

He nods in recognition. "I know you are right. But you must be careful voicing such views."

*Still a year and four months later*
*Oban, Scotland*

Some days after the dinner, they are sitting in the Plague's private room. He is one of a dozen people living in the compound who has a private room. The room testifies to the high standing he enjoys in the community. He takes out some homebrewed wine that tastes disgusting and sits down to indicate that he wants to have a lengthy confidential talk with her. An uneasy feeling sneaks up on her. She feels that maybe he wants to convince her and her daughters to stay in the compound for good. She snaps out of the feeling when tasting the wine, making a face of distaste. He laughs loudly.

She decides to convince him to flee with them before he gets a word in. That will punctuate the dilemma before it arises. She pleads with him, "You must come away with us. I beg you. There is a place out there where the war does not rage havoc. We will be free and safe there. Please come with us. For your own sake."

It seems as if he knew she was going to broach this proposal. He listens carefully and nods, accepting. "I understand that from where you are sitting, this world seems scary," he reasons, "but look at my life!" He opens his arms and looks around the room. "I have a good position and enjoy a good life."

She tilts her head. "Anyone who lives in captivity cannot have a good life," she says. "You know that! You must feel the urge to leave. To see the sky again. To feel the sun on your face. To feel the wind in your hair. To feel the wind stroke your cheek. To hear the birds. To hear the gentle noise of rattling leaves whispering in the wind. Do you never wish you could live that again? Are you willing to resign from life entirely?"

He looks down. "Of course I want all of that! Just hearing you say it makes me wish to live it again. I am sad beyond words at the thought of not living these beautiful experiences again."

He is stressed and distressed. She senses this is not the first time he has thought of escaping. He continues, "We have wrecked the world. Suspicion, hatred and greed have devoured the world. There is nothing left."

She replies, "That is true. The world has become so complex and complicated. No one understands what is going on. We don't even understand what started all this and why it keeps going. But the world still has beauty. The sky is still out there. The sun is there. The birds. The forest. The ocean. It is all there. There are still people out there that love. Give love and take love." She pauses. "They only tell you how terrible the world has become to keep you in here." She looks him in the eyes. "They forget to tell you about the beauty of the world. Keeping you scared and suspicious is their way of holding you all captive in this hidden underground world. Love and life will open you to the world. They need you to stay closed and confined. To stay scared of the world."

He looks at her. "I know you are right." He gets up and starts walking restlessly around the room. Suddenly, he turns to her. "We need to be careful," he says. "You are too reckless. Too outspoken. Such behavior will get us all killed." He looks up at her. "Do you understand what I am saying?" She nods.

Before they part that evening, they agree that the Plague will investigate places of safe haven in secret. "I have promised Atlas that we will go to Bali," she says and continues, "you can come with us. Please consider this when you do your investigation." She senses that he is equal measures scared and excited at the prospect of fleeing.

In the days that follow, they share a secret that ties them closer. "What is going on with you and the Plague?" her daughter, Rocket, confronts her.

"Nothing!" she replies. She knows her instant denial will only strengthen her daughters' belief that something is going on. But she cannot share the upcoming flight with them at this point without putting their lives at risk.

After a couple of weeks of investigation, the Plague concludes, "I want to go back to Argentina." He continues, "In fact, I insist on going back to Argentina." He looks at her with intensity in his eyes. "I still have some family there, and the country has almost entirely escaped the war. It has become a sanctuary for free factioneers from all over the world. It is the place for us to go!"

"Okay." She says contemplatively, "I lived in Buenos Aires for five years. It is a great city." She looks down. "We have one big problem. I told Atlas we would go back to Bali. In fact, *I* want to go back to Bali. I hear the island has also escaped war. I may still have my house there."

"Look," he replies, "I know you have a special bond or pact with Atlas. I have relentlessly tried to find his sister and her boys online, but there is no sign of them anywhere. My sense is that they are also free factioneers. They could be anywhere! If you want me to continue to help you and escape with you, we need to go to Argentina. You can go to Bali afterwards, if you want. But it will be without me!"

After another couple of days, he asks her, "Do you have a plan for how to cross the Atlantic?"

She looks at him, somewhat astonished. "Why should I have such a plan?" They both think. They are in the subterranean garden. Fresh water is drizzling down the walls. The air is fresh and moist. She senses that if she does not come through now, the whole escape will fall to the ground. "Of course I have a plan! You know me." She looks at him with a sly smile. She explains that she has an ex-father-in-law, who has reached a leadership position in the Freedom Fighters. "Are they not the ones roaming about just above us?" She points up.

"Yes, they are. But they are many places. All along the Atlantic coast of England and on most of the former British Isles. Further inland, Prosperity rules. It is the perfect storm, but we are safe down here… as long as we stay down here!" He smiles to her, as they both know that they will not stay there for much longer.


*Fifteen years earlier*
*Miami, U.S.A.*


She was married to X's son for eight years during her twenties. Her ex-father-in-law had since helped her when she was stuck in Miami. She had traveled to Miami during the early 2020s when Argentina went bankrupt. At the time, Miami was the only destination people could travel to from Argentina. The country had shut its borders to prevent mass immigration. She knew she did not want to stay in Argentina, given the country's dire straits.

Her mother called one evening, while she was in Miami. She was clearly upset about her daughter's life deterioration. She appreciated her mother's concern, but she didn't know what to do about it. At no point did the thought occur that she should actually come home to Denmark. "Why don't you come home?" her mother pleaded, "You are not able to work or do anything in the U.S."

"I want to come home, mama," she said, her eyes welling up, "but I can't afford the flight."

Two days later in the middle of the night, her phone rang. "Meine Schwiegertochter kommt home jetz!" It was her ex-father-in-law, and he was giving her an order.

His secretary called the following day to get her details for the ticket. The secretary explained that her ex-father-in-law wanted her to come home via Frankfurt. She was invited to stay at his house, as he had something to discuss with her. She flew to Frankfurt. She was relieved to be back in Europe. Solid ground under her feet. Finally.

As she entered the house, her ex-father-in-law ushered her into his office. He was busy but briefly explained, "I have had enough with you wandering aimlessly around the world. You are coming home and staying put till you have figured out what you want to do with your life!" This kind interest in her well-being sprang from a mutual respect and admiration. When she had married his son many years ago, she had played hard ball negotiating the prenuptial with the three lawyers representing his family. She was lawyer-less herself. She got a really good deal, and her ex-father-in-law had smiled when he realized it.

Eight years later, when she walked out of the marriage with a suitcase and a moving box, she had never claimed anything. The prenuptial was to protect her future children. She could protect herself. It was this and many other things that had made the ex-father-in-law grow fond of her. He made no hiding of his wish for her to come back into the fold.

"I have been seeing your son in Miami," she said. In the middle of all the other things that went on during the past six months of doing nothing in Miami, she had rekindled – in a platonic way – her relationship with her ex-husband, who oversaw the Latin American operations of the global family business. He was in

Central and Latin America, and nowhere specific. Whenever he invited her on a date, he stayed at the Mandarin Oriental at Brickell Keys, which was a two-minute walk from her studio apartment.

One day, he was running late. "Just go to the hotel and give them my name, and you can hang out at the pool, have some lunch, a treatment, whatever you want!" he proposed. She accepted his kind invitation, even though she felt like an imposter. This happened more and more frequently. As long as he picked up the tab when he eventually arrived, the hotel management was fine with the arrangement. But she never overdid it. She never booked a treatment and only went there in connection with seeing her ex-husband.

Hell broke loose when her ex-husband found out that she had told her ex-father-in-law about seeing him. "How was I supposed to know this?" she asked herself. Apparently, the father–son relationship had deteriorated since she had left the family. Also, she appreciated why her ex-husband was upset, since she had not told him that she was leaving, nor that his father was funding her exit. She had not told her ex-husband that she was totally broke.

*A year and five months later*
*Oban, Scotland*

She asks the Plague, "What should we do about Atlas? He will not come with us to Argentina. I promised him to look for his family and then we would all go to Bali."

"I don't know," the Plague says. He looks reflective. "Maybe we shouldn't tell him the end destination is Argentina?"

"I don't like to lie to him. Atlas and I have traveled together since the early days of our wanderings. He has always had our backs and I, his."

She decides it is time to tell Atlas of their forthcoming flight. "I will not go to Argentina!" Atlas stomps on the ground as he says it. "Why would I go to Argentina?" he continues. "At least here in Europe, I have a chance of finding my sister and her sons. Or I could go home to Bali. I have nothing to do in Argentina."

She puts her arms on his shoulders and lifts him lightly. "That is not true! You have us. We need you! We are your family. And you will have freedom. Is that not what we all want!"

On further days of reflection, Atlas decides that he will escape together with them and go with them to see her ex-father-in-law, who goes under the name "X" in the new world. Nevertheless, Atlas is not ready to commit to coming to Argentina. But he does want to leave the compound. "Maybe X can help me find my sister. Anyway, my sister is not here, and I don't want to stay here without you and Plague," he reasons.

The Plague tells Atlas and her that he has located her ex-father-in-law. "X is on the Isle of Wight," he explains. He is cheerful but continues to explain with caution in his voice, "It is true that X has a leadership position with the Freedom Fighters. We still need to travel for weeks to see him. As soon as we surface, we are in danger."

She gets an idea. "Maybe I can write him and ask him to meet us here or nearby," she says. She pushes the Plague aside, sits down at his laptop and starts writing a mail to her ex-father-in-law:

*Dear X,*

*You know me from another world. Another life. I am your ex-daughter-in-law. Married to your younger son. I have often thought of you, my ex-husband and the rest of your family. I think about you with love and gratitude. I was fortunate to have you in my life and to have you help me steer toward my purpose. Now I need to ask for your help – once again. My daughters and I are free factioneers, and we are looking for a safe passage to Argentina. Can you help us?*

*Yours, eternally grateful*

She presses send and days of waiting commence, until one day, news from X arrives:

*Dear Daughter-in-law,*

*Of course I remember you. I still have vivid memories of the old world and my family that I have all but lost. My new wife, Artemis, is my life companion and my only consolation left in life. We are unfortunately childless.*

*You ask for my help. I am in a privileged position to sit on the management committee of the Freedom Fighters that I proudly co-founded. I can offer your safe passage if you and your daughters join us and become Freedom Fighters. You will become guests of ours and protected by myself and my wife. In that case, I will send some men to bring you safely to me and my wife.*

*Sincerely, X*

Days of correspondence pass. She explains that they are only interested in a safe passage to free faction land, such as Argentina. First, she asks X to send some soldiers to meet them near the compound. When he declines, she proposes to meet someone he trusts halfway to help them navigate the rest of the way to him. "These are not unreasonable requests," she exclaims when X repeatedly refuses to help her. "What does he have to lose?" In the end, she is just asking to travel in his name as protection. "Can you please provide us with a letter stating that we travel in your name?" she pleads.

"No. My association with free factioneers will put my family and me in danger. I have power, but I also need to tread with caution," X responds. "In any event, such a letter will not grant you the protection you are looking for." He refuses to help her, her daughters and fellow travelers.

Finally, he offers that they can come see him on the Isle of Wight, if they are able to make the journey on their own. He promises that they can stay with him and work out something of mutual benefit for the onwards journey once they sit face-to-face. She is clueless as to what he is referring to by "mutual benefit," but they decide it is the best offer standing and accept it. "Maybe when he sees me in person, and we can negotiate in peace and quiet, he will help us with a ship and a safe passage out of the port," she says in hopeful anticipation. "He certainly has the resources and the power to help us."

*A year, five months and one week later*
*Oban, Scotland*

Late that evening, they sneak out of the compound the same way they entered. Along the water, they cling to the rock-hard surface of the cliffs. They slowly move further and further away from the compound. With each step, she sighs with relief. She knows that if they are caught, they will suffer the same destiny as the people whose brains they ate at the celebratory dinner in the great hall. They move slowly along the rocky coastal trail for several hours. They do not speak. All concentration is channeled toward holding on to the cliffside with their bare hands and carefully placing one foot before another on the narrow, uneven trail. The waves reach up toward them from below. Before long, their clothes, skin and hair are moist with saltwater. The cold water penetrates their bones and bodies, making them weak.

They decide to make camp for the night around midnight. By now, it rains with sleet. Their cheeks are burning with frost. It is sub-zero freezing. "We cannot stay down here by the ocean much longer," the Plague reasons. "We may not get caught, but we will freeze to death before dawn if we stop to sleep here. It is too dangerous. We need to move upwards and sleep in the shelter of the trees."

They know that above them, war and lawlessness reign. The Freedom Fighters have a stronghold along the land of the Atlantic coast. As they were unable to reach an agreement with X, they are unprotected. She wonders if she should have accepted X's offer to join the Freedom Fighters. "It would have saved us now," she whispers to herself in regret. Further inland, Prosperity reigns. Frequently, the two declared factions engage in direct combat. They always fight each other online. Intercepting online information. Feeding fake news. Yet, free factioneers fall prey to everybody. They are momentarily protected by the night and the forest. The wind sweeps through the forest like an ocean wave in the sky. The treetops bend one by one, in awe of the mighty ocean wind. She looks up, asking, "If there is a God, please help us now."

Once they are above the cliffs, they find themselves in a dense forest of wind-battered trees. A thin layer of white snow covers the forest bed. As they enter the forest, the wind silences. She is grateful for the tranquility of the forest. The forest and its creatures protect her and her daughters. "I wonder if the forest creatures are here," she thinks to herself, "or has war forced them to flee?" Just then, she feels something loving, softly caressing her burning, icy cheek. "Thank you," she whispers in deep gratitude. In that moment, she feels a warm light inside of her.

The warmth gives her a short burst of energy. "Come, girls. We will soon make camp. We are almost there." She knows from experience that in extreme situations where there seems to be no point of departure, giving up and giving in to death seems like a sweet, welcoming relief. It offers a welcomed end to all uncertainty and suffering.

They wander along a small path to an abandoned cottage that grants shelter for the night. Without speaking a word, they enter the cottage. They are exhausted as they collapse on the floor.

*A year and six months later*
*Along the west coast of England*

The next morning, they are awakened at six by men shoving them hard and talking loudly. "Get up! Get up!" They are captured by Freedom Fighters. All five of them. She is so scared that she freezes. She looks intensely at both her girls, right into their eyes, while she reaches out to stroke their cheeks. She tries to stay calm to reassure them that everything will be fine. "We will be okay. We will be okay," she repeats, as much to calm herself.

They walk through the forest in a long row. Their captors thrust them at regular intervals to make their presence constantly known. Deep in the forest, they are reeled into a hole, which was formerly used for wild animal entrapment. They lie, freezing and shivering. A toad is trapped with them in the shaft. It too cannot get up. She just sits and observes it. It is big. It is ugly. She wants to save it, but she doesn't know how. Suddenly, blankets and bread fall from above. "Look, girls! Someone wants us well. In the middle of all this, someone is helping us." She turns to them with tears in her eyes. "We will forget this terrible entrapment. The future will be good."

Three men come to reel them up out of the hole first thing in the morning. Once they are out, their captors shave their heads. She weeps. She knows what this means. Shaved heads are the trademark of slaves. Before long, they will be sold as slaves. She weeps as she watches her daughters' long golden hair fall to the ground. They all weep for the new destiny awaiting them. "Put this on," a man orders and throws a bundle of clothes on the ground.

They put on the sheetlike long gowns. "What will happen to us?" she asks, trembling uncontrollably. She is frightened. Her daughters are terrified and cling to her arm while quietly crying.

They enter a large clearing in the forest, where a hundred people are waiting. All the women and children are lined up lit de parade. They weep and shiver. This is where they will be sold into a life of thralldom. Once, they become slaves, it will be impossible to avoid this destiny. They are sold as a unit, which she is deeply relieved about. An elderly man purchases them for an uncut diamond and some cryptocurrency that is immediately transferred to the leader of their captors.

The elderly man, by the name Phaethon, rushes them onwards. He is impatient and annoyed. Once they are away from the crowds, he says, "Let's get you out of here! I bought your freedom for your ex-father-in-law." She looks at him in total astonishment. He continues to explain, "He could not come here himself, because he did not want to raise suspicion through links to free factioneers. You stupidly declined his offer to join the Freedom Fighters. That would have saved you all entirely." He is clearly annoyed with her.

She is overwhelmed with joy. "I am so grateful. This is amazing. Thank you. Thank you…" She kneels involuntarily in an act of gratitude.

"Don't thank me," Phaethon says in a dry voice, "thank X when you see him."

She raises her head in vivid alertness. "Will you take us to see him?"

"Yes. But stop asking questions. I need to focus on how to get back without causing suspicion. You need to act and behave like slaves. Otherwise, we will all get caught. Do not speak to me in public."

"Yes," she lowers her head, "I understand."

She and her daughters live in a barn, while Phaethon stays in a guestroom in the main house. There are several slave women and children living in the barn. She recognizes a couple of them from the marketplace. She and her daughters console the women as they cry themselves to sleep at night. The young children seem unaware of the horror awaiting them. The older children are in shock. They suffer in silence. The children still with their mothers console their mothers with loving pats on their heads and kisses on their cheeks. "How can these children have such a reservoir of love and compassion in this situation?" Ranger asks Rocket and her.

"I think they are trying to hold on to the essence of life. It gives them a sense of normalcy," she replies, while her eyes water with the thought of many of them being separated from their mothers soon.

As she composes herself, she turns to her daughters and commands, "Do not tell anyone that our freedom was purchased."

"Why not?" Rocket asks. "Maybe we can help some of these women and children once we get to X."

Ranger concurs. "Maybe X can help them!"

"We cannot help the whole world," she replies firmly. "We

need to focus on saving ourselves. We are not free yet. We are not safe yet. Our own freedom is all we should focus on right now!"

One of the slave women cries while saying, "I will never see my son again. He is just twelve years old. They pulled him out of my arms and put him with the men. He is just a boy. He has never been without me." The woman is inconsolable. She is speaking while sobbing, which is something that only people who have experienced extreme pain are able to. The woman asks them with hope in her voice, "Do you think I will see him again?"

"Yes," she replies. Both she and the woman know she is lying. In this new world, the only rules are the rules of war. No one questions the destiny or life of free factioneers. The declared factioneers perceive the free factioneers as lawless. They perceive them as slaves.

They stay in the barn for a few days. They await transport to an unknown future. Each day, more and more women and children depart. One morning, she gets word from one of the other slave women that the captured men will be sold the following week. Phaethon comes to them every morning in the barn with warm bread and tea. That morning, she says, "I have heard that the male slaves will be sold next week."

He looks at her with curiosity. "Yes… And?"

"I need the Plague and Atlas to be bought free as well. Please!" she whispers, making a pleading gesture with both hands. "Do not see this request as a sign of my ingratitude. I am truly grateful. But I have made an oath to them. We pledged that we will always help and have each other's back. I must free them."

Phaethon shakes his head. "You are making this very difficult. X bought your freedom, but he will not buy off your friends. This is an unreasonable request. He wanted to reach an agreement with you, which you declined. Still, he has come to your rescue. Don't you forget that!"

She knows he is right. Why should X help her free her friends when she declined all his offers? "Did I make a mistake not accepting any of his offers?" she asks herself. She is ashamed of feeling superior at the time of corresponding and negotiating with X.

She is at loss as to what to do. She turns to her daughters. "We must save the Plague and Atlas. I cannot let them down now. Still, we also need to save ourselves. My greatest obligation is to you two. I cannot call upon us the rage of X."

Rocket asks, "Can you use your own money to purchase them?"

She still has some cryptocurrency in MetaMask. All cryptocurrency is more or less intact. Banks shut down in the early days of war, and the money in the banks has all but disappeared. She recalls when Argentina went bankrupt in 2001. The government cleared all banking saving accounts. Since first-time buyers had to make a substantial down-payment on their first home purchase, a lot of her contemporary friends lost all their hard-earned savings.

Many young Argentinians lived at home with their parents well into their thirties because they needed to educate themselves, get a well-paid job and start saving for a home for their future families, all of which takes more than a decade. Only once young Argentineans were able to purchase a home could they start a family. It was a predicament that most young Argentinians and their families accepted. Nevertheless, the deep-rooted injustice of Argentinian society revealed itself when the privileged class was given a heads up by the government and was able to clear their savings accounts and move their assets out of the country ahead of the bankruptcy, while Argentinians saw all their hard-earned savings confiscated by the government.

Today, the situation where people lose all their savings and assets is commonplace. Consistently, hackers try to steal people's savings in the lawless internet. She has fought off all attacks till now. "You are right," she replies to Rocket. "I can spend my own money to buy off the Plague and Atlas." Upon further reflection, she ponders, "But to our captors, I am just a slave myself. My head is shaved. I cannot bid on them without raising suspicion and causing problems for Phaethon and X."

She asks Phaethon if he can purchase the Plague and Atlas on her behalf. She will pay with her last belongings. When he denies her proposal, she says, "We will not leave knowing the Plague and Atlas stay here, captured as slaves." Phaethon finds himself in an impossible dilemma. On the one hand, he does not want to get entangled in the situation. On the other hand, he must bring her and her daughters safely back to X. Finally, he agrees to do her bidding but not without considerable sighing and grunting.

They are rejoined and rejoice the following week. The bond between them grows stronger. They make their way south toward the Isle of Wight.

*A year and eight months later*
*Isle of Wight*

The climate on the Isle of Wight is positively warmer. It is wonderful. The warmth seeps through their bones. It permeates their bodies. This is the first time in years that her body is truly at ease. In an existence where most of life is lived outside, climate is crucial. People live better and longer lives in warm climates.

X's house is an expansive one-floor complex in limestone. The house soaks up the pale-yellow-and-pink light of the sunset. She gasps as she sees its beauty. They are hurled in through the staff entrance. "Give these travelers some food," Phaethon yells as he enters the kitchen.

The woman leading the kitchen turns around and nods. She raises her brows as she realizes that the travelers have shaved heads. "These are slaves," she says.

Phaethon moves across the room toward her. "They are X's guests. X purchased their freedom because he knows them from his 'old' life. That is all we need to know."

The woman puts her hand on her shoulder. "Let's get you all sorted. You look hungry and tired." She looks up at her with compassion. The five of them are seated at the large dining table in the busy kitchen and offered warm soup and bread. There is an eternal open fire burning in the middle of the kitchen. Afterwards, they are shown to their rooms, where a warm bath and bed await them.

The next morning, they are taken to see X. She is shocked to see how much he has shrunk in stature. He was never a tall man, but now he is very small. His body bears the marks of lifelong trials. He moves slowly across the large room toward her and the daughters. "I am so happy to see you are well," he says as he hugs her.

"Thank you for saving my daughters and me from a lifetime of thralldom." They talk at length about families, the war and how they both ended up in their current situations. "You have done well for yourself. But your losses were substantial. I am sorry for those," she says. Sitting down she puts her hand on his arm and looks him in the eyes to show her sincerity in the only way she can. They get up and start walking the grounds around the house. A small town, adjacent to X's housing complex, is in the making. New settlers are coming in as they speak. Settlers, slaves, warriors, merchants, craftsmen, travelers and diplomats are buzzing around the small town.

"I have a proposition," he says as they retire to a private room after dinner.

"Yes?" She moves her chair closer to his.

"I am getting old. My days are numbered. I need a successor. Someone who can continue the Freedom Fighters in my name. I have lost my four children in the war. Today, only their bravery lives on." His eyes well up.

"How can I help?" She does not quite understand what he is getting at. She feels with him.

"You want to continue your journey to Argentina." He turns at looks inquisitively at her.

"Yes…"

"But without a ship you will never get there. I can offer you a ship in return for one of your daughters. I have my eyes set on Ranger."

She sits back in the chair, looking out into the room in utter shock. "I cannot accept that. There must be another way."

"I am sorry," he continues, "I have bought you as slaves. If we are unable to reach an agreement at this point, you will remain slaves for the rest of your lives. Once I am gone, a new owner is less likely to treat your daughters with the care I am offering."

She gets up and makes her way to the door. "I really don't think this will work. I must think about it."

The only constant in the war is the family unit, even though hardly any families – if any – remain intact. Almost all elderly and weak people have died. Anyone incapable of walking great distances every day will eventually die. Death is celebrated as the gateway to heaven. Earth is hell. Yet people do not commit mass suicide, because no matter the hardship on earth, the joy of spending time with loved ones gives people the will and strength to continue living. Nevertheless, some people, even young infants, have nobody left in their families. A person without a family is a person without a foothold in life.

She withdraws to her room. Within a couple of minutes, her daughters knock. "Mother, we overheard the conversation you had with X. What can we do? How can we help?"

"There is nothing you can do. The proposition is impossible." She looks at them. "This is not your problem. I will try to think up some alternative. Maybe we must flee again. I am sorry." They sit and talk for several hours. This is the first time in ages that they feel momentarily safe and at ease to talk at length.

Ranger says, "Mother, if the only way we can all be free is if I stay here, then I think we must consider it." They hold each other in a tight embrace. They have such close-knit love that the thought of breaking it up hurts in their bodies. Her head is imploding with the thought of losing her daughter.

The next day, the three of them plead with X, "Is there no other way we can work this out? What if we stay here, the three of us as free people?"

"You know very well that if Ranger's mother is here, she will not be my natural successor. Then she has her own family. I must present her as my own child. My adopted child. I must present her as my true successor and rightful heir."

That evening, Ranger comes to her room again. "Mother. I have accepted my new destiny. I must stay here, so that you, Rocket and the others can become free. We cannot stay here, all three of us. This is not a bad destiny. The Freedom Fighters represent a lot of good in life. They are building a good society that I can help shape in our beliefs. The beliefs that I embrace because of you." Tears are falling down her cheeks as she speaks the unspeakable. "I will go and tell X tomorrow about my decision. This is not your decision. This is my decision." She falls to the ground with sorrow and relief after Ranger has left her room.

"You will take care of her?" she begs as they pack food, clothes and other necessities for the long sea voyage. X is letting them take everything they need for traveling.

"I will take care of her as if she is my own flesh and blood," he reassures her. Ranger is standing behind them, resolutely trying to keep her calm. Trying not to give in to the pressing tears.

Since Ranger told X of her decision, she has been under constant surveillance. X must be suspicious of what her mother may do. When they embrace, all three, to say goodbye, they weep. She is trying to pull herself together enough to give her daughter important advice for her onwards journey. "Try to forget your old life. Everything from now on will be good."

Ranger walks with them to the ship. The ship is docked the furthest away in the port to avoid unwelcome views and questions. It is a large ship, with both engine and sail. "We have been unable to get a lot of fuel for the ship. Use the sails as much as you can," Phaethon says. He is clearly moved by their imminent departure.

She pulls her daughter close and whispers, "I will be back for you in three days. Meet me in the marketplace at the corner closest to the port in three days. Come alone!"

Ranger looks down, to make sure her face does not reveal her excitement. She does not want to raise any suspicion from

Phaethon or any of the soldiers constantly keeping her under surveillance. "I will try," Ranger hurriedly whispers. "I would prefer if you just went. You know that X has tracing devices on the ship. He will kill us all if we do not stick to the plan. Or worse, we will remain slaves for the rest of our lives." She shakes her head. "Please, just go!"

The next morning, they prepare to say their goodbyes. Ranger walks with them to the port again. She is followed by a slave woman and two soldiers. X and his wife, Artemis, are also coming. On the dock, she takes both her daughters away from the group to have intimacy. She opens her arms, embraces and kisses Ranger as she says, "I will miss you forever. I will love you forever."

Ranger looks at her with teary eyes. "There is no forever. We will find each other again," she says. The two twin sisters, who have been inseparable for sixteen years, sob as they say their goodbyes.

She turns away. She is sick with hurt. Her spine is hurting. She can hardly walk upright. "How can this be happening!" she screams inside of herself. "How did I make this happen? I will never be able to forgive myself."

As soon as they stop waving, she turns to the Plague and Atlas. "We need to search the ship for tracking devices. As soon as we have turned off all devices, and we are out of sight across the horizon, we will turn around and fetch Ranger." She looks at them with piercing insistence in her eyes. "I have arranged to meet Ranger in three days."

"I am not sure this is a good idea," says the Plague. "We will all get caught and remain in thralldom for the rest of our lives."

Atlas agrees. "We are on the path to freedom now. I gave up finding my sister and her boys. We have all made sacrifices to be free."

She turns to them. Furiously, she insists, "I spent all my last savings and belongings to purchase your freedom when you were captured as slaves. Now you do not want to risk your freedom for the freedom of my daughter!" It was because of her that the Plague and Atlas were free. It was because of her that the Plague and Atlas are traveling toward a future in freedom.

The Plague and Atlas look at each other. The Plague says, "You are right. We must all stick together and have each other's backs. That is the pledge we made." They spend a day trying to find and turn off all tracking devices before they turn the ship around. They know that there is a real risk that turning off the trackers will raise suspicions with X. It is a risk they decide they must take.

After two days, they anchor the ship at a beach in a natural bay hidden by high cliffs. They need to stay hidden. If word gets out that they have returned, X will know why. They will be captured and punished. They have no time to waste. "Atlas, will you come with me?" she demands. "The Plague is staying behind to watch Rocket and the ship."

From early morning, on the third day, she is sitting in the meeting place at the market, where they agreed to meet. She is nervous. "What if Ranger is unable to make her escape? What if they have a program or trip planned for her that day? What if she has been taken to another settlement far away?" Her thoughts race around in her head. Her head hurts. "What if my daughter is unable to forgive me for the most terrible sin in life? Trading my own freedom for my daughter's freedom!"

In the afternoon, her daughter appears. A veil covers her shaved head. X says her shaved head lies about the great destiny that awaits her. She pulls the veil over her face and sits down next to her mother. "I will not come with you." She reveals her eyes and looks into her mother's eyes. "You know I must stay here. There are Freedom Fighters everywhere in the world. They will find us. They will kill us." Ranger pauses and signs, "X has already announced that he has found his long-lost daughter. People greet me with open arms. If I disappear now, he will face accusations of lying, fabrication and manipulation. He will become revengeful. My life here is not bad. It will be a good life." They both cry quietly, when Ranger says, "I will miss you forever."

They sit there holding hands for a while. Ranger says, "When he is no longer in this life, I will look for you. I will come. I promise. Put the tracking devices back on so that I can find you." She shakes her head, dismissing Ranger's proposal. Ranger insists, "You must go now. You must put the tracking back on. I will find you one day."

As she gets up to leave, her mother grabs her hand. "I cannot leave you before you have forgiven me."

Ranger replies, "There is nothing to forgive, mother."

"Yes, I have committed the most terrible sin."

"I will not forgive you for a sin you have not committed," Ranger insists.

"Then, please," her mother pleads, "I will not let you go before you bless me."

"I bless you," Rangers says with tears rolling down her cheeks. They part.

# The Journey



*Two years and one week later*
*Crossing the Atlantic Ocean*

She returns to the bay. She is devastated. Destroyed. "How could I have given away a daughter to save myself?" She repeatedly beats herself with blame, as if the loss of her daughter is not enough punishment in and by itself.

"Where is Ranger?" Rocket looks bewildered. "We must go back and get her! Why didn't you bring her?"

"She does not want to come. She says that we are not safe anywhere if she runs. She must stay to keep us out of harm."

In the following months, both Rocket and she become increasingly reclusive, sad and angry. They are angry with the universe at the inexplicable and unreasonable loss of their daughter, sister and dearest friend. She is unable to sleep. Every time she closes her eyes, Ranger appears. It is too hurtful to see her when she knows she will never see her again. She tries not to go to sleep. Instead, she is sitting on the deck looking out on the starry night – every night.

She does not like water. The ocean makes her feel unsafe. She does not like that she cannot see what is below her. She is an earthy person. She can do anything as long as she has solid ground under her feet. All people have an element. Some people are water people, like her brother, who swam with white sharks, or air people, like her sister, who jumped with a parachute alone when she was just sixteen years old.

She thinks of all the people she has lost to the war. Her brother, her sister and their families. Her dearest friends. She is angry. Rage is rumbling inside of her. But she knows she must continue. She must remain open and positive for Rocket. "I cannot also ruin her life," she convinces herself. Rocket lost her sister. She lost her daughter. She looks out at the night sky. The stars are clear and blinking. "One star for each person I loved and lost," she sobs, holding her hands to her eyes. That moment, she feels, Ranger is looking at the same starry night sky. She is looking at the same stars. They are so far away from each other, yet so close. They are alone, yet together. "Ranger must be feeling alone and lonely as well. She has no one left to comfort and love her." They both feel alone and lonely. Recognizing and accepting that we are all alone and sometimes lonely is one step along the way of reconciling with whom we are.

*Still two years and one week later*
*Primarily in Europe and the U.S.*

Populations do not receive sufficient unbiased information. People get most of their information from online feeds bolstering what they already believe. When they voice their views, all they hear are echoes reinforcing those very same views. Algorithms manage the online communities. Algorithms shape and sharpen ideologies. The algorithms and online communities become more and more polarized by the feeds. They feed on extremes. Information is scarce. Information is biased.

Corruption is widespread. Vested interests keep the truth from populations. Such interests represent the global class of politics and business. Withholding the truth from populations is coupled with scarce and biased feeds. In the end, most people belong to an online community to which they feel greater affiliation than to their fellow countrymen and women. People walk around in a haze in the real physical world, while real engagement and interaction occur online among the likeminded.

This is the backdrop of the third world war.

As the allies seek to defend friendly countries from invasion, it becomes clear that the enemy is both within and outside every warring country. There are groups within each country that are friendly with the allies. There are groups that are friendly with the enemy. Countries are being infiltrated from within. The allies try to avoid bombing these friendly groups. And yet, as these groups do not congregate anywhere specific other than on certain internet sites and platforms, the only option is to send encrypted warnings to the groups through their sites and platforms. These warnings, however, are often intercepted by the enemy. As are the bombs that are intercepted and rediverted back to the sender. There are also groups on allied ground that support the enemy. The enemy is everywhere and nowhere. The ally is everywhere and nowhere. One cannot see with the naked eye who is enemy and who is ally.

Certain countries recognize they cannot win a war by military force. But they can win the war by being the first mover of technological superiority. By infiltrating enemy populations online, irreparable internal divisions and polarization bring populations to the brink of chaos and eventually civil war. The online world is being weaponized. The digital sovereignty of nations is challenging the sovereignty of nations. In cyberspace, the war becomes a war of minds. A war of ideologies. Friend and foe become invisible. They move in the shadow of the internet.

The whole thing is chaos, and, in the end, war is waged with everybody, everywhere. To recognize allies and enemies in the real physical world, people develop signs that they use to greet each other. A raised hand or hand sign makes known the side they are on. This is risky business, because such a sign is just as likely to provoke an attack as it is to protect you from one.

*Almost three years later*
*Buenos Aires, Argentina*

When they arrive in Buenos Aires, they do not know that years of journey lay ahead of them.

Argentina is so isolated from the world that the country, once again, manages to stay out of world war. Instead, it has become a safe haven for people who have means and ways of getting there. She lived in Buenos Aires many decades ago, for five years. She recalls these memories with warmth.

At the time, she noticed that the population mainly consisted of former European immigrants that came during the First and Second World Wars. There were German Jews who fled the prosecution and concentration camps of the Nazis. There were German Nazis that fled prosecution and punishment for their war crimes after the Second World War. As both groups were German, they mixed and grew up together. They went to the same German schools. It was an unintended union of a divided population.

When she arrives in Buenos Aires, she goes every day to Iglesia de San Francisco to watch people pray. Often, people are sad. They bring a family member to console them. She watches the interaction between family members. She listens carefully to the language to see if she can pick up bits and pieces. It is easier

59

to learn the language if you couple words with strong emotions. The church is full of emotions.

The streets are riddled with potholes and the sidewalk is uneven. Cables hang above the street in a thick, supersized human spiderweb. Every time someone needs electricity, they pull a new cable from somewhere. Sometimes cables fall, and men in uniforms appear and put them up again. There is no plan. Only damage control. Like her life. No plan. Only damage control.

*Three years and five months later*
*Buenos Aires, Argentina*

They need to vacate the ship because the long and strenuous cross-Atlantic journey has wrecked it. It is in dire need of restoration. They arrange to rent an old warehouse from the port administration, which also provides a docking station for the ship. They move their belongings to a deserted warehouse in the port within walking distance from the ship. The warehouse is huge, dark and damp. The contrast to the tight and warm confinements of the ship is staggering. "At least we have solid ground under our feet," she says as she turns to Atlas.

"You *would* like that!" he replies and smiles. "You hate the ocean, its violence and unpredictability. Do you like these clammy quarters better?"

She doesn't. "We have to do something to make this our home," she continues, "We will stay here for months. Maybe years!"

As the months pass, more and more people visit them. Some of the people stay at length. Some of the people settle. "Where do all these people come from?" Rocket asks. Rocket has lived

60

her whole life in Europe. Most people in Europe are in the declared factions. In Europe, free factioneers were scarce. They lived in hiding from the declared factions. Here, free factioneers are everywhere and out in the open.

"This is a free country," she explains. "The war has not reached this part of the world. People have not been forced to choose sides. They are born and live as free people."

"This is why we came here," the Plague says, "to become free. The free factioneers in the hole were turning into a declared faction. They had the same systems and structures as the declared factions. People were punished with death for leaving. Freedom is dissolved in systems and structures, control and monitoring."

After three months, the warehouse is no longer oversized for them. They have grown to about a hundred people. Atlas explains that most of the people have nowhere else to go. They have fled random missile attacks in other cities and countries. Many of the people come from Brazil, where sporadic fighting has become prevalent during the last year.

One of the women, called Aspect, was a community leader in a favella in Porto Alegre. She is short, slightly overweight and speaks fast in a loud voice. Every morning she wakes her community group. "Get up! We need to get to work!" They have created a massive vegetable planting system in the warehouse that consists of countless drawers of fertile soil where tomatoes, cucumbers, potatoes and other vegetables are growing.

Every morning, she and Rocket walk over to Aspect and her growers to greet them and show them their appreciation for their hard work. "Morning, Aspect! How are things this morning?" she asks.

"We have a problem." Aspect turns around to face her. "Every day, we have more and more mouths to feed. We are not enough growers. How can we recruit more growers?"

"Right." She ponders and turns around to look at Rocket for an answer. "I can see that is a problem. Let me try to talk to Rocket, the Plague and Atlas to find a solution. We will come back to you with a solution." They also have livestock in the warehouse that the people of Asunción brought along.

"Look, guys," she says to the Plague and Atlas, when she and Rocket get back. "We need to talk about a division of labor." Rocket is listening in on the conversation. "The growers from Porto Alegre are working like slaves, while others are doing nothing. We all benefit from the fruits and vegetables of the growers. We should all help them grow and produce food."

Atlas concurs. "Yes. It seems like a few people are doing most of the work for everybody else."

The Plague says, "Yes. There are so many tasks. I am constantly asked to find lost ones. Communicate with other free factioneers. I am stuck in front of the computer every day. I cannot also grow vegetables."

"That is why I am saying we need a division of labor," she insists.

Rocket intervenes. "Does that not sound like the kind of society we just fled from?" Rocket looks at her mother and continues, "I mean, I understand we have a problem, and we need to find a solution. It is not fair on the growers of Porto Alegre nor on the farmers of Asunción – or any other group carrying the brunt of our existence. But if we make a division of labor, we are creating systems and structures like in the hole or like the declared factions."

"She is right," Atlas says. "We just traveled thousands of sea miles to escape the hole. Now we are pigeonholing everybody and creating a new hole."

"Let's think about it," she says. "I need to go now. The general from the municipality is waiting for me outside." She turns around as she walks toward the entrance of the warehouse. "This is my job. Minding the authorities."

The man from the municipality is a former general. She has dealt with him before in her former life. He still has the bequest of the army behind him. Army members and their families also enjoy settling on faction ground. If the faction satellite is bombed, the army members risk having poison released from the chip as a punishment for failing to protect the satellite. If the faction satellite is bombed, declared factioneers and army members become homeless. With the chip incorporated, they have nowhere else to go.

She is treading with caution. "How are you today?" She smiles at the general. If she shows insecurity, he will leap at her and swallow her. It is alarming that the municipality is sending the former general every day. They are threatening her with the general. She wants to bypass the general and go directly to the municipality. But she is scared that bypassing him may provoke his anger, followed by severe punitive consequences. She lifts her head. "How may I help you today?"

"We are being very tolerant in the city with this settlement," he starts.

She intervenes. "Yes. We appreciate that. It also helps people off the streets and keeps them somewhere safe, where they are fed and cared for."

"Yes, yes, yes. Let's not start that conversation again. I don't have time for this." He gets angry. "All I am saying is that you have to stop multiplying. Growing in numbers. I can see with my naked eye that you are becoming more and more people every day. More and more waste, noise, turbulence, chaos... The city will not tolerate this for much longer."

She lowers her head. "Yes. I realize that. We appreciate what the city is doing for us. We are not the ones encouraging people to come here. They come here of their own accord."

As she walks back into the warehouse and toward the Plague and Atlas, she shakes her head. "This is such a mess. I am telling you, we are sitting on a ticking bomb. The city will not tolerate us for much longer. We are too many. We attract too much attention." She turns to Atlas. "Did you tell everybody that they should stay in and around the warehouse? That they are not allowed to go out and loot?"

"Yes, of course I did. But you and the Plague still need to explain to me how this project will avoid turning into the hole. Systems and structures. Division of labor. Constraining orders…"

It is not the first time in her life that she has had an encounter with the general. She met him many years ago. At the time, she was trying to get her permanent visa for staying in Argentina. The general was sent to help her. It seems a lifetime ago. Today, as country borders have deteriorated, there is no need for visas. People wander the world.

*Eighteen years earlier*
*Buenos Aires, Argentina*

The general was extremely tall. She wondered how he fit into the small sports car. His torso was compact and short compared with the long legs and arms that were all over the place. He spoke in a loud voice and commanding tone. She was almost scared of him. Her boyfriend had explained that the former general would help her get a visa. Apparently, the former general was on the payroll of the American company that employed her boyfriend, an arrangement that seemed to work well for both parties.

"Get in the car!" he commanded. The car was old and worn, but he had cleaned it for the occasion. They drove downtown at an uncontrollably high pace. She did not like it. It was not the speed she didn't like but the lack of control and seeming disregard for what was going on around them. The general was not the kind of person you told what to do. She tempered herself.

A sigh of relief came to her as they rolled up in front of the beautiful colonial-style yellow building of the Migration Authority, coined the Hotel de Inmigrantes. It did a poor job hiding its dark past. Inside, thousands of Peruvian, Bolivian and other immigrants swarmed around aimlessly. The atmosphere was like a pressure cooker, tense, aggressive and hostile. The general towered over everybody. She sensed how people feared him as he slid his way through the masses like a sharp knife cutting through fresh flesh.

They entered a beautiful high-ceilinged office. At the end of the massive room, a small fat man was seated at a large desk. Another man was reclining over him. The general charged into the room as if he owned it. For a while, all three men were talking in raised voices, gesticulating with their hands in the air. She didn't understand a word and had no idea what was going on. After a while, the general marched out of the room. She followed.

They went to the basement. In the basement, there were hundreds of short, dark immigrants. In all the corridors. All the rooms. Inside and outside. They got lost in the maze of corridors and rooms in the basement. Finally, the general found the room he was looking for. He stopped, knocked and opened the door. All in one fast movement. Two nurses yelled for him to step out. After a short while, a nurse opened the door and waved them back into the room. She needed to get a blood test. They took a small sample. Once the nurses realized she was the rare AB blood type, they insisted on doing another test. Only this time, they filled a large tank with her blood.

She felt the room zooming out of perspective. She started declining to the right and eventually hit the floor with the heavy deadweight of her unconscious body. "Wake up! Wake up!" The nurses slapped her face.

She burst into tears. Not because she was sad or shocked. More in default. "Where am I?" She wet her pants.

The general looked at her in utter dismay. "Can't you get a blood test taken without fainting and wetting your pants?"

Once she had gathered herself, she looked upon a massive tiled wall full of blood containers. Hundreds of blood containers. "You are tapping and selling the blood of immigrants!" she blurted out. The general lifted her off the chair and carried her off out of the room.

"That was quite a scene you made in there," he said.

"I'm sorry. I was totally unprepared for them tapping so much blood. I have low blood pressure." She felt mildly ashamed.

"Let me take you home," he replied. They did not exchange a word on the trip back.

She ran up the stairs. "Shit, shit, I will be late." She was going to meet her ex-father-in-law at the Palace Alvear Hotel for lunch. She put on clean knickers and trousers and ran out of the door.

Walking into the gilded hotel lobby with massive chandeliers, she ran up to the receptionist and asked for the room of her ex-father-in-law. She knocked on the door. She felt uncomfortable, like she was inappropriately trespassing the personal boundaries of herself and her ex-father-in-law. "Come on in!" he yelled. He didn't seem to mind her presence in his hotel room.

"Do people forget that hotel rooms are bedrooms?" she thought to herself. "Why would I possibly go into the bedroom of my ex-father-in-law?" He was on the phone and waved her to sit down.

After ten minutes of smiling politely to her while he was talking on phone, he hung up, walked across the large room and gave her a hug. "Let's go down for lunch," he exclaimed. She was happy to see him, even though he didn't fit into this life of hers. There was a strange juxtaposition between the place and the person. They just didn't seem to match.

"Why are you here?" she asked with curiosity.

"I have a business meeting this evening," he said, "and I am visiting a production facility." Her ex-father-in-law cleansed and sold blood. She told him about the terrible incident at the immigration authority earlier that day. Before they parted, he asked, "Do you want to come for the dinner tonight?"

"Sure!" she said, not thinking anything odd about the invitation.

She wore a black dress and high heels. The hostess showed her to the large round table, where everybody was already seated. "I am sorry if I am late," she whispered to her ex-father-in-law as she sat down.

The atmosphere was tense. Nobody spoke a word. "You are *not* late," her ex-father-in-law said loudly. "We just met earlier to discuss some business." The evening passed. Nobody talked to her. They were all middle-aged white men in dark suits. She felt out of place. She didn't really understand why her ex-father-in-law had asked her to join. "Tell us what you experienced today," her ex-father-in-law suddenly said in an inquiring tone of voice.

She looked at him, confused. "What do you mean?" she whispered. "The incident at the immigration place?"

"Yes!" he replied loudly and looked around the table. She told the story as an anecdote, using elaborate wording and gestures. She wanted to entertain this thoroughly boring bunch of gray men. But no one was amused. As she got further into the story, she noticed how the men around the table exchanged looks, and her ex-father-in-law looked positively smug and self-satisfied.

She was in total shock. She had been ambushed and abused. Her ex-father-in-law now had the proof he needed to reveal that the blood he was purchasing from the Argentinean authorities came from unknowing and unwilling immigrants. "He now has ammunition to press them on the price," she thought as she headed back to her apartment in the cab. She didn't care much about this. It was all a world apart from hers. She had fled it all. The high life and high stakes. "I wonder if these men will lock me up for uncovering their scam," she thought for a second before going to sleep. She was too well connected for them to touch her.

*Three years and eight months later*
*Buenos Aires, Argentina*

There is no other option but to formalize division of labor. One evening, the three of them turn to the large main room in the warehouse. The Plague addresses the crowd. "We have worked with you over the last seven days to identify who is doing what in terms of growing and producing food, receiving newcomers and keeping the place orderly, restoring the ship, submitting paperwork to the municipality and connecting with the outside and so on. There are so many tasks that must be done every day." He looks out to sense the atmosphere. "We have decided to form seven main task groups. Each group has a leader that you are asked to report to first thing tomorrow morning."

They walk around the room, giving numbers to every single person. "One, two, three, four…" they say as they point their fingers at every person. There is a wave of mumbling in the room.

A young man gets up. "Hold on! This is a free faction! Now you are forcing us into labor. Are we to become your slaves?"

The Plague turns to the man. "Right now, we are your slaves. We are growing and producing the food you eat. We are keeping the city authority at bay. We are helping newcomers. We are helping you find lost ones AND SO ON!" The Plague raises his voice. "Do not talk to me about slavery."

She gets up, trying to calm the crowd. "In any event, if you do not like the arrangement, you are free to leave before tomorrow morning. That is what the free faction is all about. You are free to stay. You are free to leave." The next morning, the outspoken young man leaves with a following of about fifty people. A group of about two hundred stays. She is relieved. Mutiny is not a fight they have the resources to fight.

That morning, when she meets the general, she says, "I would like to warn you that we had a break-out group of about fifty people that rebelled against us last night. This group left us this morning."

"What? What a mess!" He yells at her, "The whole point of tolerating your presence here is that you keep all these wanderers in one place and largely out of trouble. Now we have a break-out group wandering around somewhere looking for trouble!"

"Please see this as a service I am doing for you," she pleads with him. "I am warning you about a particularly rebellious group that left this morning and is looking for a new place to settle."

"Not in my city!" the general exclaims and turns around to make a swift exit.

*Four years later*
*Cariló, Argentina*

Some months later, they all feel the weight of coordinating activities in their free faction community and warehouse. She is exhausted by her daily encounters with the general, who is growing more and more angry, resentful and unpredictable. The Plague says, "I did not come here to set up a new community. I need to go to Cariló, where my family and I lived before my mother and I left for Europe. If I am lucky, my family is still there. Otherwise, maybe someone knows where they have gone." "We will come with you!" she says and grabs the arm of Rocket. "Maybe there is shelter. Maybe we can settle there. We can escape the mess we have created here," she says with irony. She smiles.

Deep inside, she knows she is doomed to a lifetime of constant moving and continued homelessness. "How can I ever settle anywhere when I am missing one daughter? I will always feel homeless no matter where I settle." By now, the endless wandering has become their lifelong condition. The lifelong condition of the free factioneers. She and her fellow travelers see no other viable way of living. The lack of possessions has cemented a life of freedom, free of physical possessions weighing them down.

Word traveled of their imminent departure from Buenos

70

Aires port to Cariló. They sail on the newly refurbished ship. A group of about a hundred people followed them along the coast by foot. One night, she is sitting on the deck looking up into the stars. The stars are so much clearer close to the poles. "I wonder if Ranger is looking at the same stars right now," she thinks and remembers that it is daytime in Europe. "We are no longer looking at the same sky." Her voice descends into silence. She has never felt so far away from her daughter before. She has even forgotten her smell, while her voice is ebbing out.

They arrive at Cariló. She loves the eucalyptus trees. Together with the pines, the burning sun releases a wonderful scent. The trees lend their shade to them. They walk toward the ocean. The beach is vast and expansive. Bright white sand reflects the intense sun. "This is why I do not like the beach," she thinks. "There is nowhere to hide." The ocean is violent. Huge waves break close to land. She is dwarfed by the waves. She feels tiny.

There is no one in the ocean. It is much too dangerous to battle with these waves. "The ocean goes steeply down into massive depths," Atlas explains. It goes both high up into the sky and deep down into the abyss.

She fears the ocean. "At least on solid ground, you know where you stand," she reasons.

"What are those strange ships out there?" she asks.

"They are Japanese whalers," Atlas replies. "That is why the stern of the ship opens to haul up the whale. They chop up the whale right then and there."

She is sad. She feels like crying. "Is whale fishing not illegal?" she inquires.

"Yes, but these ships are not here," he concludes. Argentina is infiltrated by corruption on a monumental scale.

"What is on the other side of the ocean?" she asks.

"What do you mean?" Atlas looks at her, confused. "What country is on the other side?" she insists.

"There is nothing. It is a vast ocean," he waves his hand out into the open air, "but if you continue, you get to Africa."

Her eyes are welling up with tears. She feels so alone. So far away from home. "What are we doing here?" she whispers to herself.

*Still four years later*
*Cariló, Argentina*

About a year after their arrival in Argentina, war erupts in Buenos Aires and its broader region. It washes across the city, weighing it down with dense tension and fright. At first, it appears as small, insignificant waves. People hold their breath. Later, the entire brunt of war appears with the full force of mass destruction. The war is between local affiliations of the Liberators and the Patriots. These local insertions are getting support from strongholds of the Liberators and the Patriots based in North America. Other smaller declared and free factions are involuntarily engulfed in the war. Before long, the entire city and region are turned into a battlefield.

The people in power have their own interests in keeping populations in a haze. Populations have limited or no access to decent jobs, housing, education, health and other basic amenities. This life situation creates desperation and aggression. Yet by shutting down, ridiculing and alienating certain opposing groups, people feel they belong. It reinforces the "us and them." The resistance from opposing groups fuels them. It gives them a life purpose. Their comradery and togetherness gain strength from resistance. The harder the lines are drawn up between the Liberators and the Patriots, the more difficult it becomes to unify communities.



*Still four years later*
*Cariló, Argentina*

They decide it is best to move somewhere else. Along the west coast of Latin America, peace still reigns. They prepare to flee – again. By now, they have grown from four people to a group of about a thousand people. All of them are free factioneers. All of them want to find a place of sanctuary. "Go to the ship and get the trackers," she says to Atlas. "My daughter must be able to find us no matter where we go."

They move slowly by foot toward the north. The ship follows them around the South Pole. In certain areas, particular factions start to congregate. The movement of factioneers shifting across the continent to reach friendly ground adds to the chaos of war. Enormous movements of factioneers, seeking refuge in what they have read online or heard word-of-mouth are friendly grounds, are in the making. Sometimes, when a movement of thousands of factioneers enters a so-called friendly ground, the area has since been taken over by the enemy. People keep moving. As no area declares colors nor has the means of claiming land, it is impossible to know who is where and where to go.

"Sir!" Phaethon calls X to the screen waving his hand. "They are moving! They are not moving across the water. They are land-borne. But the trackers are moving with them. How is that possible?"

X looks at the screen. "She must have found the trackers and brought them along on the trip. She wants to be found. She wants to be reunited with Ranger one day."

Four years and two months later<br>
Cusco, Peru

They arrive in Cusco after two months of walking. The city is impressive. It exudes history. After decades of war, historical markers have become a rarity on earth. With the colossal stones of the Inca Empire, the Spanish built their homes in Cusco. These homes represent the defeat of the Incas. But they also represent a continuation of history. We can never run from our history. History is built, stone by stone, of each of our collective experiences and memories. We are all insignificant when perceived on a global and historic scale. Kings, queens and presidents come and go. It is the collective – not individuals – that creates history and memories. We each feel that our own life is the most important. But we are all just tiny pieces of a giant puzzle that is shaped and reshaped on a continuous basis. We may play a role individually, but it is all the pieces put together that make up the puzzle.

She wonders why people would delete events and change the narrative of our collective history and memory. Surely, removing a few stones will not change the collective memories of what we have all lived through together. We can add to history. Discover new stories that have not yet been told. But we cannot delete history. Instead, we must embrace history, talk about it, understand and learn from it. Some history must not repeat itself.

Each stone of the Spanish conquerors' homes represents an action or memory in time. If you remove a stone, the house crumbles. If you remove a stone, history and the opportunity to learn from it disappears. Erasing history prevents us from understanding and learning from it. We can add but not remove nor delete an action or memory in time.

When she was in Cusco last time, she went to Machu Picchu. She has vivid memories of the impressionable trip.

*Eighteen years earlier*
*Machu Picchu, Peru*

One day, she gets the idea to go on the Inca Trail to Machu Picchu. Machu Picchu was the last bastion of the Incas before they were finally wiped out by the Spanish in around 1550. Machu Picchu was built in around 1450 and is hidden away almost eight thousand feet up in the Andes Mountains.

Always one to make plans on the spur of the moment, she decides to join a group that is leaving the following morning for Machu Picchu. There are few organized trips. She grabs the chance. "Do I need some kind of equipment or special clothing?" she asks the leader of the traveling group with desperation in her voice.

"You do not need equipment, but you do need appropriate clothes."

"Where do you get that at this hour?"

"You can go to the market of Clara Maria." She runs out of the door in search of the market of Clara Maria.

There are absolutely no appropriate clothes to get at the market. It is all foods and home utilities. However, she manages to find some clothes in alpaca, the local cloth fabric made of fur from llamas. It is dirt cheap. The next day, she turns up looking like she is going to a costume ball. The other travelers are dressed in fancy, expensive westernized tracking and climbing clothes. She also only has a tiny rucksack with a couple of items, including a toothbrush. The other travelers have protein bars, extra clothes, first aid kits, torches, blankets and other practical items.

The terrain and weather change radically during the course of one day. They start in a tropical forest and before lunch they are walking along small, barren, steep mountain trails in the burning sun. By afternoon, they are above the clouds on the mountain peaks in what is essentially a blizzard snowstorm. All along the way, travelers move at different speeds. At the mountain peaks, they stop to make fire and wait for everyone to catch up before they proceed. She is freezing. The carriers are tiny, extremely strong men. They carry everything from a stove to heavy crates on their backs up and down the mountains. They are faster than everyone else. They take mercy on her and lend her a blanket.

The evenings are pitch dark. You can hardly see your hand before you. Without a torch, she is obliged to wait at the fire till everybody has left for bed. Then she picks up a piece of firewood or burning candle to light her way back to the tent as the only source of light on the dark mountain back.

The last day, they get up at four in the morning. They have to make it to Machu Picchu by noon. In the pouring rain, she climbs the final trench up a slippery stone wall with her bare hands holding onto the cliff. She does not look down because she knows it will cause her to lose her grip.

She returns to Cusco by train. The train is a historic relic. It is a steam locomotive; the steady pumping rhythm calms her. It makes her profoundly content and happy to sit in the train as it curls its way back through the mountains to Cusco. Women are selling wonderful homemade food that no foreigners dare touch for fear of stomach disease. She is acclimatized to the continent. Whenever she moves to a new country, she knows that a terrible bout of illness awaits her. Rather than sheltering herself from local germs and diseases, she invites them to home her body and mind. By now, she is resilient.



*Four years and three months later*
*From Machu Picchu, Peru, to Lima, Peru*

It is with a heavy heart that they depart from Cusco after a couple of days' camping. "The ship will be in Lima in a couple of days," the Plague continues, "we cannot stay here. We need to get to Lima to meet up with the crew and the ship."

Atlas says, "I heard that we could get a bus to take us to Lima in just two days. Should I investigate that?"

"Yes please!" she says and folds her hand in a pleading gesture. She is exhausted from the walking.

"But we cannot get buses for everybody," Rocket says, concerned. "What do we do and say to the people we are leaving behind?"

The Plague responds while he is looking down at his task. "We will tell them that we need to get to Lima in a hurry to make sure that the ship can dock… That is the truth." They decide to offer pregnant women and women with small children a lift with the bus.

"Do not think of any dangers when traveling on a bus across the mountains and great plains of Peru. The bus driver has driven this route a million times before," she thinks and asks herself, "Why should it go wrong this time, when it has gone well millions of times before? Have faith in faith." The bus carries too many people. Once it moves out of Cusco, people leave the bus and are replaced by chickens, goats, lambs and even a small calf. Chickens manage to break out of their cages and start fluttering around the bus. Everybody works together to capture them and put them back into their confinement. Four-legged animals have their legs tied together and are swung over the backs of their owners. The smell reeks of dirty, wet animals.

The women's dresses have a particular feature. The dresses are very wide and floor-length. They are, in fact, quite beautiful and colorful. A woman sits next to her. The woman's dress lays over her tights, and she feels the wetness of the dress penetrate her trousers. She tries to carefully remove the dress, but the woman gets noticeably displeased with this gesture, so she stops and resigns herself to dirty water penetrating her clothes. In Peru and Bolivia, people don't like to be looked at. She looks out of the window intensely to put her surroundings at ease with her being there. For hours, she looks out of the window.

The bus stops randomly where there are people waiting or where passengers ask to get off. The great plains are one of the most beautiful landscapes she has ever seen, on the same level of beauty as the Nile River in Egypt or Oban in Scotland.

The great plains are a luscious green with high grass waving in the constant and hard wind. People's faces are wind-ridden and red. A strange monotonous noise emerges from the wind. A small gathering of people in beautiful, bright clothes stand in the high grass. It is the welcoming of one of their own. The bright clothes seem to fit naturally into the bright green environment. There is a sense of total harmony between people, culture and nature.

The bus drives onto a wooden raft as they prepare to cross Titicaca. Titicaca is an immense lake in the high plains. The bus swings from side to side in the wind and high waves. She holds her breath until she lets go to take in the experience in full. On the other side of the lake, a large festival greets her. Probably a couple of hundred people are gathered for some kind of festive event. The bus driver decides to join the festival. The bus does not continue till the next day. Unlike in the 'old' western world, festivity occurs without alcohol, which removes a lot of the unpredictability, tension and violence that former westerners grew accustomed to, especially in their nightlife.

It is the celebration of the liberation from the Spanish conquerors. The celebration includes a horse getting a condor fixed to its upper back. Surface holes just below the mane are made and the condor's claws are inserted into the holes. Every time the horse jumps and kicks, the condor opens and flutters its wings. Its claws penetrate the fresh wounds of the horse. The condor represents the Peruvian people and horse is the Spanish conquerors.

She knows this is animal cruelty, but she also knows when to keep her mouth shut. This is not the place nor the time to make any comments. Instead, she decides to observe and view it as an artistic performance. Later, when she arrives in Lima, she passes a café in the evening and by total coincidence she realizes that they are showing a movie about how the condor is captured for the celebration. A horse is tied to the ground on the great plains. Eventually, the horse starves and the condor descends to eat its dying prey, like the vulture. At this point, the condor is caught in a net and carried away to partake in the performance.

*Four years and four months later*
*Lima, Peru*

The ship is already docked at the port in Lima by the time they arrive. The ship has become their steady base and home. They are all overjoyed to reconnect with the crew and the ship. They sleep on the ship the first night. "The ship looks in a pretty bad state," she says to the captain the next morning.

"You don't want to know how trying the trip around Cape Horn was," the captain says. "There were a couple of times I thought we wouldn't make it."

Lima is a wonderful return and revival of old memories. She traveled extensively in Latin America when she lived in Argentina for five years.

"The Patriots' satellite has been hit!" The man delivering the message looks equal measures upset and excited.

"We need to find out if this is true and what it means," the Plague says. He leans forward and looks at her as he continues, "This could mean that thousands, hundreds of thousands of people, are homeless. They are without a community. It will be extremely disruptive to world order."

"I am not sure we can call the current state of affairs 'world order,'" Atlas says in a dry voice while he continues reading.

"It could also mean that more people will become free factioneers," she says, hopeful, "now they have tried the declared faction life, which is rigorous and tough." She looks out on the group of free factioneers that has settled with them in an old and abandoned Lutheran sailors' church in Lima port. There are about a hundred followers. "Maybe we will become stronger in numbers from this disaster. Maybe some of the former Patriot followers will want to become free factioneers. I mean, they cannot join the other declared factions, as they are not welcomed." In fact, when a satellite is hit and a faction implodes, all factions want to welcome these newly homeless people, as it strengthens their own faction by numbers. When a faction satellite is shot out of the sky, the venomous chip is put out of order, which opens up the potential for new opportunities of allegiances.

"I wonder who shot the Patriots' satellite out of the sky," the Plague says.

"Let's confirm if this is true before we get all excited," Atlas says, while still reading. The Plague and she have become unofficial leaders of the hundreds of free faction travelers. Atlas has no interest in becoming a leader. Since they came to Buenos Aires, he has become reclusive. At times, he is bitter and even resentful, blaming her and the Plague for giving up on his search for his sister and her boys. Yet, his more anonymous status enables him to mingle with their group of free factioneers. He picks up and passes on gossip and messages to her and the Plague.

"Why don't you try to find out if this is true?" She turns to Atlas. "Try to find out what people are saying. Where does this news come from?"

*Still four years and four months later*
*Across the world*

There is little means of verifying the information released on the internet. There are just anonymous people posting true or fake things on the internet that gain momentum. Politics of war is waged, and opinions are swayed on the internet. People are effectually walking around in the online minefield, seeking refuge in the real world. The enemy could be the person walking next to you. In this way, what started as a war between nations imploded into a multitude of civil wars. Nation states broke down.

High tech war has taken to space. In space, there is no loss of human lives. Just vast material loss. Satellites are launched by certain declared factions. The satellites are critical to hosting the internet communities and platforms of different declared factions. When satellites are bombed out of the sky, factioneers become homeless. Homeless factioneers do not receive warning signals nor other crucial information. They live in a cyberspace vacuum. In the real world, they wander aimlessly around. In this state, they become vulnerable prey to other factions. With time, homeless factioneers sign up to other affiliated sites and platforms and thereby enter a new faction and regain a new home. They receive signals and information again. When a satellite is bombed and its members sign up with a new faction, former allies suddenly become enemies and former enemies become allies. This adds to further confusion and chaos.

The satellites that are kept afloat the longest grow the largest following. They host the largest factions. The satellites are owned by extremely wealthy individuals or global corporations. Satellite owners are called satelliteers. The satelliteers' main job is to protect the information on their satellites. This information includes the anonymous names and phone numbers of all faction members. One satelliteer can hold information on more than one faction, but waterproof shutters are kept between factions.

Unfortunately, oftentimes, it makes more sense to bomb an affiliated satellite than an enemy satellite, as the factioneers signed up for the affiliated satellite are more likely to redirect and sign up to the factions hosted on affiliated satellite rather than factions on an enemy satellite. Therefore, allies are also bombing each other's satellites to grow their following. The goal is to grow the number of factioneers. The satelliteers don't manage the content of the sites and platforms they host on behalf of the factions. They only keep the satellites afloat – together with the warlords. The content stems from random anonymous factioneers. The power of the factioneers shifts depending on who posts, what is posted and how many likes it gets. War is waged by either bombing satellites out of the sky or by hacking satellites and accessing factioneer information, spreading malicious information and viruses.

*Four years and eight months later*
*From Lima, Peru, to Quito, Ecuador*

They move by foot from Lima to Quito across the highlands. By now their numbers have swelled. They are like a swarm of grasshoppers leaving a trail of destruction behind. They eat everything that is edible along on their path. They loot to feed hungry stomachs. They do everything necessary to survive. On the one hand, life on earth resembles the very first settlements of human existence: the hunter–gatherer society. On the other hand, the presence of technology permeates society and renders new opportunities for borderless monitoring and control.

The blacksmith returns to play a central position in any civilized settlement. He makes all weapons, ships and carriages. Women have taken up weaving clothes. Farmers, hunters and craftsmen play essential roles in these new societies.

They arrive at Quito early one morning. Nature has devoured the city. It is cold. The hazy fog dampens the noise of the hundreds of free factioneers as they enter the valley. Some hundred settlers wake up and cannot believe their eyes. Some try to flee. The free factioneers try to calm the settlers, reassuring them that they are friendly. In this corner of the world, declared factions have not yet emerged. Here, the war has only recently started to rage. The people of Quito did not understand who was bombing them and why. They still don't understand. No one understands. The algorithms induce rage in certain factions against imaginary enemies. The result is random destruction by unknowns.

The city is located almost three thousand meters above sea level. It is in a pressure cooker encapsuled by a mountain ridge that protects it from the harsh winds. The air is thin, and most travelers get dizzy and lightheaded. The high altitude has no impact on her. She understands it will affect some with nausea and headaches.

She was here before in her former life.

*Nineteen years earlier*
*Quito, Ecuador*

When the plane comes out of the clouds to descend, she is shocked to see the ground right below. The city is literally right below the clouds. High up in the sky. It is sitting on a hilly landscape, with lush nature protruding through the cement buildings. She books into a hotel on a molehill. The hotel is small but very comfortable. It has dark interiors. Commonly in countries with lots of sun, interiors are dark. In contrast, in countries with little sun, such as Denmark, interiors are light.

She arrives in the middle of the night and goes straight up to her room. The next day, breakfast is entirely homemade and tastes amazing. Even the marmalade is homemade. She goes to the kitchen counter to say thank you for the wonderful breakfast. She enquires about where they got the fruits to make the marmalade. It makes for small conversation. Not because she is interested in pointless conversation but because she wants the kitchen staff to feel her appreciation. Her sense is that they do not get a lot of visitors from outside Ecuador.

After some days, she wakes up and sees total destruction outside her hotel window. For a second, she thinks she might still be asleep. Most houses are made of wood and tin. During the night, they collapsed in an earthquake slightly over 5.5 on the Richter scale. She felt nothing and slept right through it. "The night must have caused a lot of commotion?" she asks the kitchen staff. By now, she talks with the kitchen staff every morning.

The next morning, she looks forward to going home. She wants to be back in Buenos Aires in time to celebrate her thirtieth birthday. She makes her way to the airport. She has traveled for more than a month and desperately wants to get out of her one set of dirty clothes. The airport is total chaos. For some reason, there are lots of people and women in traditional clothing that she doesn't recognize.

As she checks in, the woman at the counter says, "Sorry, but Aerolinas Argentina has gone bankrupt."

"What!" Her heart is pumping. "How did this happen? Why did no one tell me?"

"Maybe they did not know how to get in touch with you. You have to pay the airport tax if you want to check in," the woman says in a dry voice. She spent all her money on homemade marmalade from the hotel. Luckily, the American businessman next to her takes mercy on her and pays her airport taxes. She is stuck in the airport for a day.

She keeps going up to the airport staff to inquire how to get to Buenos Aires. "You can take a plane to Rio," the man responds after she has chased him around the airport for ten minutes.

"But Rio doesn't get me closer to Buenos Aires," she says, upset, "It just gets me across to the east coast. It doesn't make a difference." They want to get rid of her. She needs to make sure that they get her on the right plane.

Later that afternoon, the man tells her that she can go to Lima. She had just been in Lima prior to Quito. But, at least, it will get her closer to home. Once in Lima, the whole waiting around and chasing airport staff recommences. Lima airport is next to a fish power factory. The smell of rotten fish day and night is unbearable. Airport chairs are purposely uncomfortable to discourage people from sitting there for hours and descending into sleep.

Finally, after two days and one night of curling up on a bench, an airport service employee says, "We can set you up in a hotel."

They drive her to the Hilton Hotel in the city center. It seems too good to be true. "But you are not allowed to leave the hotel," the chauffeur says when she gets off. "We will pick you up on short notice. You must be ready to go so that you don't miss the plane." For the first couple of days, she has a ball. It is great to be in a hotel with a shower, television, gym, room service and large windows overlooking the city. Time and place do not matter to her because she isn't going anywhere. If you don't know where you are going, you are not in a hurry to go anywhere. She has all the time in the world to just be.

*Five years and a couple of weeks later*
*Quito, Ecuador*

Some smaller groups dispatch to look for food and go hunting. The area is scarce of food and cannot feed all the travelers. "We have to move on before people start getting desperate with hunger," she tells the Plague and Rocket the following morning.

They nod.

"Which way?" Rocket asks.

"Does it matter?" the Plague responds.

"It does matter," she replies. "I think we should move further north. Maybe all the way to North America to bid welcome to homeless Patriots." She smiles.

"This is exactly the kind of reckless behavior you are so well known for," the Plague responds, smiling. The life of war and wandering has taught them all to grab the chances that life offers. They have become fearless.

Traveling like she did, she feels she is always in-between. She is never anywhere. Just in-between places. She doesn't need to commit to any place. She uses the travel to travel inside herself.

They need to get to North America before homeless Patriots sign up with the Liberators, Prosperity, Freedom Fighters or form another new faction. The Plague says, "If we are able to move our followers to North America, we can attract homeless Patriots to the free faction. They will be able to join us even though they have the Patriot chip, now that their satellite no longer tracks."

"I have heard that the Freedom Fighters have found a way to disconnect and extract chips," Atlas says.

She adds, "The Freedom Fighters are not strongly represented in North America. Their stronghold is in Europe. We must hurry to win terrain before the Freedom Fighters get there."

"I thought that we, as free factioneers, were not interested in this power game," Atlas says firmly and continues, "the growing by numbers. I am totally discouraged by this conversation." He gets up to leave.

She turns to the Plague. "He is right. What has happened to us? We are becoming like them."

The Plague reasons, "I still think we should go to North America. In some ways, we are offering these homeless Patriots an alternative to the declared factions. A life lived in freedom."

"You don't have to sell this idea to me. I also want us to go to North America. For now, I also want to grow our numbers. We become less vulnerable the larger we are. We become a free faction to be reckoned with by sheer multitude. Still, I think Atlas has a point."

The seeds of a potential conflict are planted. Some free factioneers cherish their freedom. Other free factioneers believe that only if they grow in numbers, organize and institutionalize, they stand stronger vis-à-vis the declared factions.

The benefit of being a declared factioneer is that you are allowed to settle on faction ground, where you become part of a society. The endless wandering ceases. To protect the declared factioneers, their families, assets and grounds, an army is created. Anyone can sign up for the faction army, which is kind of a mercenary army. The mercenary soldiers also have chips incorporated, but these chips are removed once the soldiers' term of service terminates. If a soldier leaves the faction in an untimely manner, he will die through the poison released from the chip. In fact, anyone leaving the faction, whether they are declared factioneers or deserting soldiers, will die through poison released from the chip. The poison is released when the tracking device detects unwarranted wandering beyond faction land. The poison is also released if you try to remove the chip. However, if the faction satellite ceases to exist, the chip is disconnected and cannot harm anyone. In this moment, factioneers become homeless and open to considering other options of allegiance.

As they move farther north, it becomes impossible to travel as a group. They are too many people and new people continue to join their group. People are following them. Some people have heard that she has close ties to the newly appointed leader of the Freedom Fighters, Ranger. They believe they are protected by her close ties to the Freedom Fighters. Just being in her proximity protects them from the Freedom Fighters. Some people whisper that the Freedom Fighters will come to their rescue if anything happens to them. They stay close by. They also believe that she, the Plague, Atlas and Rocket have access to secret information that helps them move forward and onto safer ground.

*Five years and one month later*
*From Quito, Ecuador, to Buenaventura, Colombia*

The war has moved from North America southwards. The farther north they move, the more intense the fighting becomes. Destruction is more rampant. People are more erratic. The situation is more uncontrollable. As they approach Buenaventura, missiles fly over their heads. She screams out at her daughter, "Rocket, come here! Come here!" She reaches her hand out to grab her daughter's hand. They run to hide from the missiles flying above their heads. "Plague! What should we do?" she cries out loudly.

"You must get to water! The missiles have heat detectors. They pick up body heat. Get under water! Now!" She and her daughter continue moving under the trees. The missiles are picking up heat from the hundreds of followers running in all directions. Everybody is scattering everywhere.

They reach a small shallow pond hidden by the low trees. She pulls her daughter into the pond. They run, fall in the water, get up and run again. "Down! Down!" she screams, "Take a deep breath and hold your breath." Others are following them into the water. She glimpses something moving out of the corner of her eye. They disappear under the thick, muddy water, hold their breath. She feels something stroking her right back thigh. She gets a shock and races to the surface of the water. Once she is above the water, she realizes that a swarm of crocodiles is getting into the water. She pulls her daughter out of the water.

"Stop! Stop!" the daughter yells, "Why are we getting out? There are still missiles!"

"There are crocodiles in the water." She points toward the water, where one crocodile is violently throwing around a human body. People in the pond start screaming and running out of the water. More and more crocodiles descend into the water. "We need to get away. We need to stay close. If we are lots of people running frantically in all directions, the missiles will not know where to attack."

After hours of confusion and running around, things calm down, and she realizes that dozens of followers have disappeared. Some of the followers have been killed. Some are lying on the ground screaming, turning and twisting in pain. They are missing limbs. Corpses have surfaced the pond and are floating in the water, tinting the water red. She weeps and turns to her daughter. "This is a bloodbath. I did this! I am responsible for their deaths. I led them down a wrong path."

Her daughter squeezes her hand and looks at her through her watery eyes. "You could never have predicted this attack."

"No. But I led them this way." She gasps for air. "If everybody had just stayed in Quito or Lima, a lot of deaths could have been avoided."

"We don't know this. The world is in upheaval. It is difficult to imagine how things could have played out differently," her daughter resigns.

She and her daughter continue their travel with the Plague

and Atlas and some three-dozen followers. "We have probably lost more than half the group," she says.

Atlas tries to console her. "They may not all have been killed. Some took a different route. Some went ahead of us and got away before the attack started."

"It is total carnage." Her eyes well up. "We are to blame!"

Atlas gets up and puts a hand on her shoulder. "We are not to blame. This is war! I presume the missile attack targeted us for coming too close to North America."

The Plague says, "The Liberators are not interested in any other faction entering their stronghold. They got rid of their archenemy, the Patriots. They are free to take over the whole continent. We need to hurry before all the homeless Patriots are forced to sign up with the Liberators."

Atlas turns around and looks at the Plague. "We need to be extra cautious the closer we get. If we continue to proceed as a large group, we'll attract too much attention. We need to act as if this one attack was enough to destroy and discourage us from proceeding."

The Plague addresses the last people still standing by them. "Our group needs to scatter. We cannot walk together. I will send information to you every day about our whereabouts, our condition, any threats, safe pockets and so on." The Plague communicates with the other free factioneers in their group via a platform they set up before they started their long journey. In each break-out group, an appointed leader is responsible for keeping up to date with faction news and communicating back to the Plague.

By the time they reach Buenaventura, she turns to her daughter and the Plague. "I think we should get on the ship and sail the rest of the way. It is much safer. I don't feel safe walking any more." The ship has faithfully been following them along the shoreline to Buenaventura.

"Give word that we will meet next time in Ciudad Juárez near the Rio Grande," she yells to Atlas while moving away and toward the port.

"When will we be there?" he yells back. They agree to meet in three months. They try to spread the word as best they can, but people are already moving.

"How can they just start moving, if they don't know where we are going?" Rocket says with despair. By now, all the break-out groups have access to the platform. At this point, the platform is the only glue sticking them together.

*Five years and four months later*
*From Buenaventura, Colombia, to Ciudad Juárez, Mexico*

The sail trip allows them to contemplate their options. "If we manage to grow a considerable following, we could settle in North America," she says to the others and continues, "War is moving from Europe to Africa and the Middle East and from North America to South America. Ironically, both Europe and North America have become relatively peaceful places."

"Yes. Peaceful if you are in one of the big declared factions," Atlas responds. "If we are just a small group of free factioneers, we will not be at peace anywhere."

Atlas looks out over the sea. "The only place we will find peace is in Bali. I know this to be true." He misses his family and home country.

She says, "If we are just a small group of free factioneers, you are right. But if we are a massive faction of hundreds of thousands of followers, we will be a force to be reckoned with. Therefore, we need to grow our following." She looks down regretfully. "Sadly, we lost a lot of good men and women at Buenaventura." She turns to the Plague and her daughter.

The Plague looks reflective. "We need to get organized. Like a declared faction, but without the entrapment. Without the chip. People should be free to leave without paying with their lives."

"You want free factioneers to sign up to the same platform? To be on the same frequency?" Atlas asks, turning to the Plague. "Should all or some of us have a tracking device? Really, sometimes you talk as if we are a declared faction." They need to get organized, but they also need to find a form of organization that does not resemble the declared factions.

Traveling by ship has done them good. By the time they arrive in the Gulf of Mexico, they are well rested.

*Between nineteen to fifteen years earlier*
*From Buenos Aires, Argentina, to Copenhagen, Denmark, to Miami, U.S.A.*

Many years ago, when she lived in Buenos Aires, the country went bankrupt. The airport was shut down to prevent people from fleeing the country. Of course, the affluent political and financial class was given an early warning and had already left the country, but for everyone else, leaving the country was treated as an act of treason. "This is when Argentina really needs you!" her friend told her with desperation and distress in her voice, when she explained that she wanted to move back to Denmark. Her Argentinian boyfriend had already moved to the U.S. She had no reason to stay and free fall into chaos with the rest of the population.

Her Argentinian boyfriend left Argentina immediately after the economic crisis broke out in Argentina in 2001. She was left

93

in their joint apartment to watch how the country and the economy dismantled before her eyes. Her company was basically bankrupt. Without her company, money or a relationship, she found herself stuck in Buenos Aires with no purpose. No purpose is usually the privilege of the super-rich, or it is the curse of the super-poor. Despite being neither, she had experienced both several times in her life. As traveling was impossible she was unable to leave the country. She was stuck in limbo. But it would get much worse.

Her boyfriend had already left. The company he worked for financed his master's degree in health finance at Wharton University. He was very ambitious. She was quite sure that part of the reason why he was with her was that she represented an exit ticket away from Argentina to Europe.

He visited her in Denmark. He arrived in Copenhagen on New Year's evening, close to midnight. She was spending time with her mother in her mother's apartment, which was located right at the city center near the New Square of the Kings. As he came into Copenhagen, he became more and more horrified by what he saw. Finally, arriving at the New Square of the Kings, his mind was pretty much made up. He did not want to live in Europe. Not after all he had seen. People from outside Europe sometimes regard Europe as one big country, despite its numerous countries with substantial national differences. In much the same way, people from outside the U.S. categorize the U.S. as a homogenous unit. The same probably goes for Africa, Latin America and all other man-made geographical agglomerations.

The New Square of the Kings is in an affluent part of

Copenhagen. The plaza and buildings date back to 1670. Commonly, people from outside Europe mistakenly think that as a wealthy country, Denmark should have beautiful state-of-the-art modern buildings, wide roads with expensive cars, and so on. Instead, the country delves in its history, which is generally well preserved.

Old roads and buildings seem to contradict the idea of wealth of people from less wealthy countries. "Why is everything so old?" he had asked her with skepticism, "Surely, if you are so wealthy, you don't have to live in old shitty buildings!" She had looked at him in disbelief. She ended up not answering, because she didn't know what to answer. She was unprepared for the question. To reinforce the "oldness" of the city that evening, people were slipping out of buildings into the streets in big, long gowns and black-and-white dinner attire to cheer in the New Year with Champagne, drunk hugs and kisses. He felt he had arrived at an absurd historic play. Copenhagen was the backdrop of this play. He felt he was unwillingly taking part in a Shakespearean comedy that ridiculed his aspirations.

After this experience, he no longer wanted to use her as an entry ticket to Europe, and their relationship started to fade. This is when he had decided that he had to go to the U.S., where he felt he could feel and taste the wealth he aspired to. His company provided a way out of Argentina, and a nice American Ph.D. student cemented his stay when they married. He had started the relationship with the American Ph.D. student before he had ended the relationship with her. Obviously, she didn't know this, but she later found out, when she was finally able to leave Miami. But first, she needed to get out of Argentina. Once flights reopened in Argentina, there were few destinations that you could go to. Miami was the only destination that was outside of Latin America, and therefore she got on that flight. Of course, she also thought that she was moving closer to her boyfriend, which seemed like a good idea at the time.

He had managed to rent a small studio on Brickell Key for her, near the luxury hotel, Mandarin Oriental, that she would later frequent to visit her German ex-husband. There was no furniture in the apartment, and she had only brought one suitcase with some clothes. She bought an inflatable bed that she put in the middle of the room. There was an echo in the room, which meant that she often got complaints about noise from the neighbors. Not because she was noisy, but because the slightest noise would echo out and amplify. The view from the studio was quite wonderful. She could see a pool below and the azure-blue ocean in the distance. Her boyfriend was paying for the studio. He was renting it from an Argentinian couple who were well settled in the U.S. She sensed that they felt pity for him and her.

She went to the Argentinian embassy one day to consult on the situation of the country and how to access her savings in the Argentinean bank. When she got there, she was totally surprised to see a large advertisement for her company that she had left behind. She had literally just left it. Walked out. She had not consulted the authorities to formally close it or anything. In hindsight, she appreciated the non-bureaucracy of Argentina that was the result of a country that had lost track of formal rules and regulations.

For instance, she had to go once a month to a small office that was highly efficient (to encourage small business start-ups) and pay whatever she wanted in VAT. Of course, such laxity could be used to cheat, but for her it just made life much simpler. When she was later in Denmark, she really came to appreciate this, as Denmark is hyper-regulated, and the authorities track and trace a citizen's every move. She felt that the Danish state infringed on her citizen's rights. If you are "fortunate" enough to live in Denmark, you must be part of the state-driven monitoring system.

She asked one of the embassy employees that had come out of his office to help her. "Why do you have this advertisement poster? Where does it come from?" He explained that the poster was to inform about a CARITAS project that her company had sponsored. She felt inwardly proud but kept it to herself. The last money she had before she left, she had given to a CARITAS project that offered single mothers a plot of land to build a house and grow some crops. By now, she recognized that whenever she reset her life, she would start afresh penniless, as she had given her last money to someone else. She was good at earning money. Holding onto it was another matter.

She recalled the CARITAS project. They had driven in a minivan for hours through favellas to get to a peri-urban rural area. Here they got out and walked the last mile across some fields. "This is it!" the CARITAS worker exclaimed and opened his arms. "This is how we spend your money. To acquire this land and divide it into smaller plots." There were already three small shacks on the land. "We are invited to take tea and biscuits."

They walked over into one shack, which was full of women and children. "Please, take a seat." The woman showed her the one chair in the room. She sat quietly and drank her tea. She didn't say a word. The CARITAS worker made a bit of small talk.

As she sipped her tea, illness crept up on her and seeped into her bones. By the time she left, she was feverish.

Six years later<br>Ciudad Juárez, Mexico

The ship anchors at Laguna Madre y Delta del Río Bravo in the Gulf of Mexico. The land is flat and barren. The beach is wide and the water shallow. They have to throw anchor far away from the coast and walk in the shallow water onto land. In this landscape, they are totally exposed. If there are enemies waiting in hiding, they are easy prey. The water seems particularly salty, leaving white rings around her thighs that she cannot brush away with her hands. She feels the taste of salt in her mouth. Her mouth is dry. The sun and heat are overwhelming. She already feels exhausted, even before they have started. Sailing offered a pleasant break from the endless walking. "I cannot keep walking like this," she thinks aloud to herself, "My legs are worn out. My back is collapsing."

Her daughter hears her and says, "I hope this is the last long journey we will be making before we settle somewhere. I think everybody is exhausted from walking. We are all looking for a place to settle." She is right.

The walk toward Ciudad Juárez will take them at least two weeks. They are walking slowly in the heat. On the water, sailing, she felt the warm breeze in her hair. The contrast to the stark heat on land is staggering. The barren landscape offers no hiding from the burning sun. The rhythm of her steps is monotonous. Step by step. Moving forward. Move somewhere and nowhere. It resembles her old life. Her life in the hamster wheel. Day in and day out the same drill. Uninterrupted, treading the wheel.

Monotonous. "At least in this life, I do not know what awaits me tomorrow. I am seeing new places. Living new experiences," she thinks.

"Are we going to make it in time?" She turns to Atlas and asks, "I mean, hundreds of people will meet us at Ciudad Juárez. I imagine that it is not without risk to gather so many free factioneers in one place. In the open landscape. Waiting there will increase the level of risk."

"I know," Atlas responds, "We must keep the pace up. Better we wait for them than the other way around."

With each day of walking, more and more free factioneers join their little group. The group grows. She is astonished by the intense pressure, desperation and distress of people. It feels like everybody has reached their limit. By the time they reach Ciudad Juárez, there is a sea of people. They live in makeshift tents. Rockets exclaims, "These people can't all be waiting for us?"

"No, I guess not," the Plague says, contemplating. People turn and look at them as they pass. They smile, nod and greet them.

Atlas says, "Now we are in real trouble, folks! These people seem to think that we can help them."

"How can that be?" she says, "What have you been communicating?" She looks at the Plague with a stern look.

"This is not my fault!" the Plague insists.

Factions are not divided by ethnicity, race or religious beliefs. In all factions, all ethnicities, races and religious beliefs are represented. Factions are determined by affiliation to certain online communities that feed information from and to their members on a constant basis. The information includes warnings about enemy movements, personal accounts of events, members' congregations in friendly areas, and so on. The members also release information about their personal beliefs, whereby the lines between "us and them" become even stronger. Such personal accounts state opinions or describe events, such as a combat with the enemy.

For almost as long as the eyes reach, there are people and makeshift tents. There is a constant buzz of mumbling. Things seem calm and under control. But underneath the calm, unrest is boiling. They sense that these people have been waiting in the camp for months. Waiting to cross what was once the border to the U.S. "Why have all these people stopped here?" She turns to the Plague. "Why don't they just walk on? There are no borders."

The Plague is as astonished as she is. "I don't know who these people are and what they are doing. I don't know why they don't just walk on."

The idea of nation states is archaic. National governments are a relic of a time long gone. Financial markets are global and operate beyond the control of national governments. Crime is global and operates beyond the control of national governments. Human trafficking and migration are global and operate beyond the control of national governments. The Refugee Crisis of 2015–2017 testifies to the lack of control that governments have. In any event, the idea that only certain people should be allowed to live in certain places is absurd. If you want to live somewhere else, why should you not be allowed to do so? Why should someone prevent you from putting on your walking shoes and start walking?

Of course, if someone just got off the train, they should not be allowed to access the same public perks and benefits as someone who has paid toward society their whole life. "Nevertheless, surely, with sophisticated systems and structures, we should be able to offer differentiated treatment of citizens rather than excluding certain citizens from certain places," she explains to Rocket, who seems to be the only one willing to listen to her rant.

They make camp. Atlas says, "We need to stay here to make sure that all our people are here. We need to reconnect and regroup before we proceed." Atlas is their conscience.

"You are right," the Plague responds, "We must make sure we are all here before we proceed." They have hardly any food, and there is no food in their vicinity. If there ever were fruits, nuts and animals, they are all but gone now.

She turns to a woman sitting next to them with three small children. The woman is black. "She must be from Brazil," she thinks to herself and asks the woman, "Why have you all made camp here?"

The woman looks surprised at her question and responds, "Have you not heard?" She widens her eyes. The black woman musters the last ounce of energy left in her. "The Liberators are trying to claim the territory that was once the U.S. They come here at regular intervals and raid, slaughter and take slaves." She looks down. "This is why we are all gathered here. We try to have strength by numbers. Before we started gathering here, people were scattered in smaller groups along the former border. We were all just sitting ducks."

"What do you do?" she asks. "What are you waiting for?"

The woman replies, hesitant, "Suddenly, people will mobilize. We will run in the thousands toward the north. Like a swarm of grasshoppers. The sheer number of us will overwhelm the Liberators."

"Right," she says and looks out over the expansive vastness of people. "But it sounds like a risky and random game of life and death. It is Russian roulette. Don't many of you get killed?"

"Yes," the woman replies. She still doesn't understand why they all want to go north.

The number of people suddenly swells when their group of followers joins them the following day. If the settlement was boiling with unrest and revolt before, now it is on the brink of explosion. "We have to push on right away," the Plague resolutely says. "The longer we stay here, the hungrier we all get. The more frustrated and desperate we get."

People constantly come up to them. They greet them. They kiss her hands and feet. She doesn't really like it. Atlas tells her, "You and the Plague have taken a leadership position. With leadership follows responsibilities and obligations. You cannot choose to opt out now. It is yours. Own it!"

She knows he is right. "You know that some of these people, maybe most of them, think I have ties to the Freedom Fighters. They think I can somehow protect them." She looks at Atlas. He shakes his head in resignation.

As the four of them get up to leave, a deep-seated, unsettling feeling creeps up on her. They look around to see that all the people in the camp are getting up to leave with them, as the black woman had explained. Thousands of people start moving. "This is going to get out of control," Atlas whispers to himself.

Within the next five minutes, a massive army seems to rise from the ground. It appears from over the hilltop. "They must have been lying in wait!" the Plague screams. Screaming, running and panic wash over the crowds, that start disintegrating in all directions.

"This strategy is a terrible strategy!" she says and grabs the hand of her daughter.

"Run north! Run north!" the Plague screams and points north. Many followers gather around them. They don't buckle.

They stay by their sides. It is impossible to move anywhere. They are caught in the middle of the crowd of followers.

She looks up into the sky. "Is there a God or has God left us? If there is a God, I need you now. I need you now!"

The Liberators' army is properly prepared and equipped. There are only a couple of hundred soldiers. But they are in full armor. They advance slowly. They are not in a rush. They are taking it all in. The soldiers use knives, daggers, clubs and stones. Some soldiers even kill with their bare hands. People are defenseless. There are cries from people falling to their deaths. Cries of small children, orphaned in a split-second. The soldiers leave a trail of blood and death behind them. The bright red blood lights up in the desert before it is absorbed into the yellow sand.

She feels a knife penetrate her left foot. She is unable to move. She is pinned to the ground. While standing there, she is beaten several times by random soldiers passing her. The pain is excruciating, to the extent that she cannot scream or cry. The soldiers batter and smash every person they pass. After several beatings, she falls to the ground while trying to call out to her daughter, "Run! Run!" But the sound of her screams is muffled.

Her daughter stops to watch her fall. "Mother! Mother!" she cries, running over toward her. Rocket kneels and lies closely against her battered body, holding onto her mother with both hands. She keeps screaming, "Run! Run!" But nobody hears her. She goes in and out of consciousness. She senses that the crowd around her is thinning in numbers as people are killed. The battle is ebbing. In that moment, she lets go and enters deep unconsciousness.

*Six years and several months later*
*Albuquerque, U.S.A.*

Someone is pouring ice-cold water over her face. She gasps for her breath. She wakes up, but she cannot move her battered body. Her daughter gets up. She is ready for combat. Two men in uniforms pull her and her daughter into the back of an SUV. They haven't seen such a car for years. She is sitting in the back of the SUV bent forwards, holding her hands on her sore, battered stomach. The bumps of the road roar up through her body. She cringes with pain. The bright red blood has dried and turned dark. Now it blends with the colors of the landscape.

A large group of slave women with shaved heads and dressed in bright orange enter the battleground. They run frantically around the ground. She wonders what they are doing, but she is too weak to speak. They are looking for something. She realizes that they are looking for infants and young children. One woman is carrying three infants on her chest. These children will enter a life of thralldom. The children are too exhausted and frightened to utter a sound. Their dark eyes reveal a deep pain, a pain that will haunt them for the rest of their lives. Her daughter looks out and shakes her head.

Out of the corner of her eye, she sees hordes of hunchbacked jackals entering the deserted battlefield. The jackals move fast. They pull out large lumps of fresh flesh from the dead corpses scattered around the ground. Soon, nobody will know what occurred here just a few hours ago. All traces of the hundreds of people will be erased in a couple of days by the jackals, vultures and other carrion eaters flocking to the field. It will all be forgotten. They will all be forgotten.

They drive for a couple of hours through the dusty desert. She feels the thick sand in her hair and on her skin. They halt at what was once Albuquerque. The city is gone. The gravel from the collapsed buildings blends with the sandy soil. Sandstorms have covered many of the ruins. They drive through high gates and into a large courtyard. Circling the courtyard are low buildings with holes as doors. There are no windows. "Get out!" one of the soldiers commands. He lifts her arm to move her swiftly out of the truck. Her daughter willingly follows her mother.

They move across the courtyard, where they enter a large room with an oversized desk that claims almost the entire room. Behind the desk, a short, overweight Hispanic man, who is the general, is sitting. He raises his head to look out over the desk into the room. "Come and sit here." He waves her and her daughter over to his desk. He seems calm and polite. "Are you thirsty? Hungry?"

They both nod, accepting his offer. "Please," Rocket says. The man waves to two soldiers for them to bring food. "You are here as my guests." He leans back into his oversized chair. "You should feel at home."

She is still exhausted but mutters, "I think I need a doctor. My foot is hurting. My body is aching."

"Of course!" He snaps his fingers toward the soldiers. One of them sets off out of the door. "The doctor will be waiting for you in your rooms. Let's take you there." He waves his hand to the last soldier standing behind him.

They take off across the courtyard again. The soldier is walking fast. She trots behind him and almost collapses. Rocket runs to pull her arm up around her shoulders. She lifts her mother into the room. Once in the room, she lies on the bed, shaking. The doctor attends to her. She gets some strong painkillers, maybe morphine, and calms down, while the doctor tries to mend her body. "Take these sedatives and sleeping pills after your bath and before going to sleep," the doctor says on his way out of the door. "You need a good night's sleep. Both of you." He points at them and looks at her daughter.

The subsequent day, they venture out of the room. They fare carefully. "What are we doing here?" Rocket asks. "Why are they being so nice? These are the exact same people who slaughtered us like cattle yesterday on the battlefield." She looks at her mother anxiously.

"I know, my love," she says and grabs her hand. "Let's just stay close and observant. We will soon know what is going on." They have breakfast with the short, overweight Hispanic man. He seems delighted to have company from the outside world. Maybe even delighted that the company is female. He is chatty and cheerful. "What is this place?" she dares to ask him.

"This is a military compound of the Liberators. It is from here we guard the border," he replies, unable to hide his smugness.

"You have borders here?" Rocket asks. He smiles overbearingly.

When they return to their rooms, they wonder for how long they will stay in the military compound. They wonder if the Plague, Atlas and other followers survived, and where they are. A slave woman enters the room. She has blond hair and blue eyes. She looks like them. "Where are you from?" Rocket asks.

"I don't know," she says and looks down. "I think we wandered down from the north. But I have been here for so long that I hardly remember my old life and the old world. It seems worlds apart."

She moves closer to the young slave woman. "What is this place?"

"It is a military compound of the Liberators," she replies.

"We know that. But why here? Is this region a stronghold of the Liberators?"

The woman is thinking. Her eyes are looking toward the ceiling. "I think so. The place seems highly protected. It is unbreakable. We have had some missile attacks, but the missiles are stopped before they enter the compound."

She looks at her daughter. Rocket concludes, "It sounds like a missile shield is protecting the place. It is probably also highly guarded with sensors. We should not try to escape."

On the way out of the door, the woman turns to them. "You are taken hostage here. You must be valuable. Otherwise, they would have killed you or taken you as slaves, like me."

For the next weeks, she and Rocket spend almost all their time in the rooms they have been allocated. There are no windows. The air inside is fresh and comfortable. Outside, the sun burns, day in and day out. Her body is mending, but the wounds of her mind will never heal. That night, she lies in bed, staring into the dark. "Do you think I should have acted differently?" She speaks out into the dark, not knowing if Rocket is awake and hears her.

"You could not have known," Rocket says, half-asleep. "No one could have known." They both lie there in the dark, revisiting the horror of events, wishing it had been a terrible dream they will soon wake from.

They are becoming restless. "How long will they keep us here?" Rocket asks in irritation. "We don't even know why we are here and what they want with us."

"I am also becoming frustrated with the waiting and not knowing," she replies. "You must have noticed that I try to get some answers from the general every time we meet?"

"I know," Rocket says, "but he is a slippery eel." In the

evening, they are picked up and taken across the courtyard to attend dinner with the general. Every evening is the same. Every day is the same. Day in and day out, for weeks.

The general is particularly cheerful that evening. "Why are you so happy?" she asks him.

"Well," he says, looking her in the eyes, "we have finally received word from the Freedom Fighters!" He claps his hands in excitement. "We have been trying to find out whom to talk to within the Freedom Fighters, which was no easy task. They are a funny lot." He lowers his voice. "They have no clear leader. They seem to have several leaders spread out across the entire world. What a peculiar set-up. Like a lot of smaller enclaves that operate separately from each other."

"Sounds wise enough to me," Rocket says. "If you have one leader, you become very vulnerable if that leader is gone. Or murdered. Then the whole house of cards collapses."

"Yes, yes," he says, "smart girl. But I have no interest in discussing the structure of the Freedom Fighters with you."

"You still have not explained why you are so excited," she insists. "Why did you reach out to the Freedom Fighters?"

"I heard from a reliable source that you two are in close kinship to their leader, well, one of their leaders. With that information, we thought we would approach the Freedom Fighters and propose a deal." He is positively beaming. "And that deal is now in the brewing."

"Are you dealing with the Freedom Fighters with us as the bargain?" she says.

Rocket concurs. "They have no interest in us! We are free factioneers, in case you haven't noticed!"

"Yes," he says and leans forward, "so you say. But for some reason, they are willing to negotiate with us." He smiles and leans back in the chair again. They realize that they will not get any more information out of the general.

Once they are back in their rooms, they are perplexed and excited. "Do you think your old father-in-law has come to our rescue again?" Rocket asks.

"No; why would he do that? We are long gone, and he got what he wanted: Ranger." They look at each other with a knowing look.

"Could it be Ranger?" Rocket almost doesn't dare to say her name.

"I don't know. Maybe," she says.

The following days are unbearable. The wait is unbearable. They speculate whether the Liberators want a ransom for them. If they are considering a hostage swap. If they will have to go back to Europe. What destiny awaits them there. The thoughts are crowding their minds. Their minds are a whirlwind of unanswered questions.

The general suddenly turns up in their quarters. "Get ready to leave!" he says. He stands with his legs widespread and his hands resting at the waist to inflate his small physical presence. "We are going on a trip. Hurry! Hurry!" Shortly after, they are sitting on the open boot of the SUV truck again. This time, the general is sitting in the front. "Hurry on! Hurry on!" he yells to the driver. Two more SUV trucks follow them, and several men on motorbikes. For hours, they travel under the burning sun. They feel how the sun burns their flesh. Suddenly, they halt at a small river. The banks of the river are green, and birds are tweeting. On the other side of the river, a small group of a dozen men and women are gathered around a fire.

They jump up as the convoy approaches and halts. They stand on each side of the river, staring at each other on full alert.

The general yells in loud voice, "Bring out the hostages!" The party at the other side turn around and run toward a small tent, from which they haul three men with sacks over their heads and their hands tied on their backs. They stumble, get up and feel their way forward again with their feet.

When the hostages are standing on each side of the river, the general yells, "Now!" They are pushed into the water, and the general waves to Rocket and her to walk into the water. The closer they get to the other side, the more the hostages pick up speed. When they get to the other side, they sigh and collapse with relief. "Get up!" a woman says, "There is no time for relaxing. We must move out of here immediately. We are on the Liberators' territory."

They move in a new sparser convoy eastwards. "We have a ship waiting for us," a man turns around to tell them, "We need to get there as soon as possible. We are not safe here."

"Who are you?" she asks, perplexed.

The woman says, "We are Freedom Fighters from the Isle of Wight. Ranger sent us to get you out of captivity."

"Does X know of this rescue operation?" she dares to ask. The woman and the man look at each other. Neither of them answers.

Night falls. It is inconvenient, yet inevitable. They must stop and make camp. They sleep below the open night sky. She looks up at the sky and the stars. "Each star for each one of my loved ones." She traces her thoughts back to when she was sitting on the ship leaving Europe. Now, she and her daughter are going back.

Rocket grabs her hand. "Mother, if they send us back, all this was for nothing. We are back to where we started. And what if X does not want us there? Will we be sold as slaves and move somewhere far away from Ranger?"

Her thoughts are with the Plague and Atlas. "Did they survive the fighting? Where can they be?" she thinks to herself.

Years later, she imagined that her miserable childhood might stave off future suffering. "Surely, God cannot be so heartless as to keep on throwing bad things at me," she thought. But terrible things continued to be thrown at her. She is aware that many of the things are of her own making. She is willing to take responsibility and learn from her mistakes.

By the time the war emerged, she had resigned herself to the idea that everybody gets their fair share of good and evil in life. She had let go of the idea that there is some kind of divine justice where the "punishment" fits the "crime." She realizes that fate seems to be a random hodgepodge of trials and blessings. "The broadest shoulders carry the most," her brother said wisely. "If anyone can handle all this, it is you," he continued. The idea that you can be in the wrong place at the wrong time rang truer and truer. Nevertheless, she also fundamentally loved life and generally remained a positive soul.

During that night, the woman who first greeted them and seems to be the leader of the group sneaks up to them. She whispers, "You should run now."

"What?" She wakes up from her thoughts and turns around to look at the woman in bewilderment. "Where to?"

"I don't know. But if you stay, we will bring you back to Europe and Ranger. She says you are better off running. She says you are going somewhere. To Bali?" She pauses and looks at her. "Ranger says that X does not want to see you. You are not safe in Europe." They get up before they have time to think. The woman pushes a heavy purse in her hand and holds her hand firmly. "Take this! It is from Ranger. Run that way. I will make sure we do not look for you, if you run that way. Anyway, we must get to our ship. We will not stay behind for long and look for you. It is too dangerous for us to stay here. I will take the blame for having lost you."

Once they are out of immediate danger, Rocket looks astonished at her. "Why does Ranger want us to run?"

"Ranger must know that we are better off not going back. Maybe we will become slaves again. In any event, X cannot be too pleased with the prospect of seeing us. I doubt he even knows that Ranger is helping us."

"She must have a lot of power to seal a deal for us on the other side of the world, in her own right."

They walk all night. "I cannot believe we are walking again," she says. "I am too old for this. I cannot stay on the run."

"You have to, mother," Rocket says with compassion, "I cannot lose you too. We will soon find a place for free factioneers. We will be safe."

"For a short moment, we may be safe," she replies with a dry voice. "Is this not why we want to go to Bali?"

Rocket looks with affirmation. "We need to get to Bali. You always said there is land out there, where we will be safe and free."

In the full breakdown of war, there is no real reason for moving anywhere, because the enemy and ally is everywhere and nowhere. Albeit, as the old Greek man said, "If you are going through hell, keep walking." People feel they must keep walking. People do not understand why they are moving or know where they are moving to. They have lost sight of the end goal. There is no end goal.

After years of wandering around interrupted by sporadic, intense fighting of different factions on the ground, people have forgotten why and what started the war. It is no longer clear who is on whose side. Everyone is in fact on the side of the internet algorithms. No one, not even the algorithms' creators, understands the algorithms. The algorithms have taken on their own life. The algorithms feed off the information entered by their members. Nevertheless, there is no way of verifying the authenticity of this information.



They move west. Walking. They need to get to the west coast in order to cross the Pacific Ocean and get to Bali. She has no idea how this might happen. They lose count of the days, weeks and months. The years. They realize that the war and constant wandering must have lasted a decade. But no one has an exact count of time. The passage of time has become fluid. Some people claim to know the date in the old calendar. Yet, there is no way of verifying the authenticity of that date. Time is standing still while moving forward at a high velocity. They are walking slowly while rushing to get away and go somewhere. She is running in quicksand. Running and never getting anywhere. There is no destination. Only the passage of time.

The new world is full of juxtapositions and contradictions. Their minds are the same. As human beings, they know they are capable of great achievements. Building a rocket to fly to the Moon. Fly through the sky to different destinations in the world. Build a powerplant to power cities of millions of inhabitants. Factories. Supertankers. Global trade. Skyscrapers. Cars. Trains. Cure diseases and mend minds. Education. Enlightenment. The list is endless. Yet, at the same time, everything has been destroyed by the very same human beings who build it all.

Humanity has been pushed back to the Middle Ages. Important applied knowledge dies with people from the old world. Some cars are still operative. She thinks that someone probably reopened an oil drill and refinement facility. But every single screw is in deficit. When something breaks, it is usually left to deteriorate. Nothing can be done at scale in this new world. There is no fuel. No energy. Only homemade wind or solar energy. Water is sourced by hand from freshwater rivers and underground sources.

The global population is radically reduced. People die due to harsh living, endless walking, combat, lack of food and lawlessness. There are also countless pandemics raging. It is unclear if the pandemics started naturally or as biological weapons against the enemy. The fact remains that once unleashed, the pandemic does not differentiate between friend and foe. Anyone with a weak psyche and physical inability is either left behind to die or has taken their own life. The new world is no place for fragile souls and weak bodies. The only winner in all this mayhem is nature. It flourishes everywhere. It rises and spreads in the most unlikely places. Earth reclaiming the earth.

As they keep moving west, the landscape changes from an opulent overflowing of nature to a barren desert. They are heading to the Cortez Sea, where hearsay has it that ships, including undeclared ships, depart to cross the Pacific Ocean to southeast Asia. After several weeks, maybe months, of walking, they arrive at their destination, Mejor Atardecer Guaymas. The place is stunning, with small islands and cliffs scattered across the bay. There are dolphins jumping in the shallow, warm water. The beach is pure and white. The houses are low and white. The sunset is breathtakingly beautiful. The irony is that the more remote a place is, the more it has retained its original buildings, beauty and inhabitants. The war targets the most populous places. Remote places remain largely intact. Unfortunately, before the war, populations congregated in the large metropolises, making them particularly vulnerable to attacks. With one bomb, whole populations were wiped out.

The ships anchor far out in the bay. The only way to get onboard is by rowing out to the ships. "Excuse me," she says, approaching an elderly woman, "I am looking for a captain. Is there a place where the ship crews hang out in this town?" The woman looks at her and her daughter and points to a small hut on the beach. They descend the narrow winding stairs and walk across the sand to the hut. Palm leaves extend above a simple wooden structure. A wooded bar and makeshift kitchen occupy half the establishment. Chairs and tables are scattered randomly below the palm-leaf canopy and beyond to the beach. It is early morning and only a few staff are there. "Who is the owner of this place?" she asks the man behind the bar.

"Rocky. He is sleeping. He will get here around noon," the man says.

"Please, let's get some breakfast," Rocket pleads. "Thank God for the money Ranger gave us!"

After breakfast, they fall asleep on a bench in the vicinity of the bar. When they wake up, the bar is buzzing with people. Once they collect themselves, they return to the bar. "I would like to talk to Rocky." Rocky is a nice-looking man with dark eyes and blond hair. The sun has left deep marks on his skin, revealing that he is older than his demeanor. She asks him if he knows of any undeclared ships going to southeast Asia within the next couple of days.

"The captain of *Aida* is a free factioneer. The owner of the ship is a private merchant, who is also a free factioneer. I think." He looks contemplative.

"Do you know the captain's name?"

"No."

"Do you know where the ship is anchored? Any trademarks of the ship that will help us recognize it?"

"It is a big ship with three masts and a large crew. We don't get that many ships in the bay of that size."

Since the breakout of war, global trade has ceased. Everything is hyper-localized despite the global presence of technology. Bartering has replaced monetary exchange and fulfills most people's needs and wants. The little monetary trade there is, is usually directly commissioned by leaders of the declared factions. There is still fictitious money swirling around cyberspace, but it is not tied to any financial institution. All institutional money has disappeared. Institutionalization rooted in the physical world has but all vanished.

Like the Argentinian government that emptied people's savings accounts to use the funds to get the country through the crisis of 2001, former governments emptied people's accounts to fund the war. Like in Argentina, where the privileged class was allowed to move their money out of the country and into safety before the government raided the banks of ordinary people's savings, some privileged individuals were allowed to move their wealth into safety at the outset of war.

The only money left in this war-ridden world is held by the privileged and the few individuals that read the writing on the wall and moved their wealth into cryptocurrencies and bitcoins before the collapse of the global financial institutions. And yet, cyberspace finances were and still are entirely global and largely unregulated. Whereas the old financial institutions lived somewhere in the physical world, cyberspace finance lives nowhere and everywhere. Whereas the old financial institutions had real people at their helms, cyberspace finance belongs to nobody and everybody. It is the democratization of finance. In this gray zone, hackers constantly raid accounts. Unlawfulness is the only supreme ruler. Trickery is the means to an end.

There was a total breakdown of global diplomacy, finance and trade. In the war, most powerplants were destroyed by the enemy. Consequentially, cross-continental trade and transport are once again fueled by wind. Again, juxtapositions and contradictions prevail. While space and satellites direct large declared factions and cyberspace directs their finances, life on the ground and life for the great majority of people has been thrown back centuries.

They walk along the beach, looking at the ships. "That's it!" Rockets says and points out a large, beautiful wood ship with three masts.

They ask some fishermen nearby what they know about the ship. "Can I pay you to row us to that ship?" she asks and opens the palm of her hand to show some gold coins.

"I'll take you!" one of the fishermen says. The closer they get to the vessel, the larger and more daunting it appears. The shadow of the ship engulfs them.

"What if they are not friendly?" Rocket asks. "What if they rob us, or worse, what if they take us as slaves?"

They are both worried. She tries to remain calm. Once they are next to the vessel, the fisherman screams, "Visitors!" They are hoisted up on a rope with hoop. She ascends first.

"Hold tight!" she insists as her daughter is pulled up. "We

need to speak to your captain," she says in an assertive voice. They look puzzled.

The captain is a tall man in his sixties. He is youthful in his walk and attitude. He moves briskly toward them across the deck. He sways from one side to another, as if the wind and waves are catching him. He seems in a good mood. "What can I do for you, ladies?" he says in a loud voice.

She doesn't answer till he is right next to her. She doesn't want the whole crew to hear their conversation. "Can I talk to you in private?" she whispers and looks him in the eyes.

"Yes, yes. What is this about?" They descend narrow, steep stairs to a large, dark room. He waves his hand for the crew to vacate the room. They sit down at the large table. Small round windows report on the bright sun outside. Yet, the sun's rays do not reach far into the room. They are swallowed by the darkness of the room.

She tries to collect her thoughts before she starts. She knows she cannot tell the whole truth. "I don't know if you know…" she says secretly, "but there was a large battle in Ciudad Juárez near Rio Grande some months ago."

"I heard of that. That was a long time ago and before we got here!"

"We escaped that battle," she says and looks up at him. He looks surprised at them. "Barely escaped," she whispers. "We have been on the run ever since. We need to get to a safe place. We are exhausted by the endless wandering." He nods and looks down. She can see he appreciates what she is saying.

During their years of wandering, she often asked herself, "To what extent am I hiding from the world? To what extent am I seeking myself in unfamiliar places across the world?" She feels the captain may share that notion.

She had to stop fighting. She intrinsically thought that any trial could be overcome by sheer will, force and persistence. In some ways, she thought that she could outfight and outrun any trial. "You cannot keep on doing the same thing," her friend had told her. "Fighting has brought you this far, but now it may be time to change your ways. To let go. Maybe that is what life is trying to teach you. To stop fighting and open yourself up to what life has to bring."

Most people think that if they pay their dues and live honestly, they will get through life happily. Nevertheless, the multitude and variation of trials are countless. Some trials are self-inflicted, which make them easier to accept. Other trials are entirely out of our hands. In all trials, there is only so much we can do.

For her, the life lesson is understanding and accepting that trials happen regardless of how she tries to live her life, pay her dues and positively confront every challenge with a go-getter spirit. Life is no longer entirely in her control. She can no longer will her way out of difficult situations. Rather, she has to surrender to those difficult situations and go with the flow. "One door closes and another opens," she thinks. "I just have to learn to accept. Keep an open mind and let the universe do its work."


"Can I pay you modestly to sail us to southeast Asia? Is that possible?" They both look at the captain with begging eyes. They would never dare to ask him if he was not a free factioneer. If he did not share their wish for freedom.

He looks back at them with a suspicious look. "I heard that a woman and her daughter are on the run from the Liberators *and* the Freedom Fighters! That is quite some achievement." He looks at them, waiting for an answer.

"We are free factioneers," she starts. "I think that is all you need to know. It sounds incredible that someone should be on the run from both the Liberators *and* the Freedom Fighters." She smiles.

He sits quietly and observes them, with his legs crossed and his hands relaxed in his lap. He tilts his head. "I don't want to get into trouble," he says, hesitant. "But if you are fine with sharing an alcove, then I can make room for you. Then you can come along. We leave tomorrow morning first thing. Doors are shut at six o'clock this evening."

They both get up in excitement. She feels like embracing the captain with joy but restrains herself. Instead, they embrace each other while making small jumps of joy. "Finally! Finally! We are going to a place of peace and freedom."

He interrupts their joyous dance. "Some practical issues…" he says. "You pay me directly for the trip. You do not tell anyone you paid for the trip. That stays between us. Instead, you say that you are my sister-in-law." He points at her and then at Rocket. "And you are my niece. Your kinship to me will keep you protected. Otherwise, you will not be safe here. You have to watch out for yourselves and *always* watch out. The trip will take about two months, depending on the weather."

"Yes! Yes!" Rocket says, clapping her hands. He continues to explain that if they need to do something on land before leaving, they must do it now. Everybody will be onboard by six that evening and for dinner at six thirty. No one gets off or on after six.

They decide to go back on land to buy some warm clothes. Maybe it will get cold on open sea at night. Maybe their rags will not make it across the Pacific. They have three hours. They need to hurry. Once on land, they ask for directions to the marketplace, where they buy leg- and arm-warmers and a sweater each. All of it is made of alpaca.

The evening sun bakes the sand-colored limestones of the gateway to the marketplace. The marketplace has survived the war and testifies to the natural passage of time. They appreciate buildings worn by time. Buildings that have not been destroyed in the war. Just before six that evening, they are once again hoisted up to *Aida*, their new home for the next two months. They are excited at the prospect of no longer being hunted as animals. No longer constantly watching over their shoulders. No longer fleeing. No longer endlessly wandering the world. Soon they will live in peace and free of prosecution. "Let's not get ahead of ourselves," she says calmly to Rocket, "We still need to keep a façade with the crew. Anyone can rat us out to the Liberators or the Freedom Fighters and earn a finder's fee. We keep our heads down till we are in Bali."

The ship seems to be in a time warp dating back to the eighteenth century and the beginning of global trade and slavery. The captain explains that they cannot sail with engines because there is no fuel. The powerplants were the first to be destroyed during the war. The ship's cargo holds cotton, corn, sugar, wheat, and so on. Most societies have returned to the basics. They have become agricultural societies. Large-scale manufacturing, container freight and ports are things of the past. Slaves that have been taken captive during the war are used for hard, laborious work in the fields. Even *Aida* has slaves.

Most of the slaves on *Aida* are former declared factioneers who lost their faction through a breakdown of their online community. "Some of them are probably former Patriots," Rocket says with sadness in her voice, "They were free until recently." Declared factioneers who lost their faction, like the

Patriots, became homeless stray dogs searching in the real world for their fellow factioneers by returning to the greeting signals used at the beginning of the war. They are captured as slaves. They are the legitimate war bounty of the war victors. Also, free factioneers are perceived by most declared factions as easy prey that is up for anyone's grab, since no faction protects them. The slaves are of *any* all races, ethnicities and religions.

A kaleidoscope of different races, ethnicities and religions is everywhere. The last decade of global migration has entirely melted the pot. The migration that was kick-started by the onset of war is entirely globalized, a reflection of the online communities that are disenfranchised from their national heritage. The online communities are blind to race, ethnicity and religion. The avatars are of any skin color, age and sex. They do not declare their race, ethnicity nor religion.

With time, online communities started to claim land and congregate in certain places in the physical world. This physical manifestation of online communities gave birth to mass migration of all people and in all directions. All people are going everywhere. It is the total breakup of national borders and nation states. Everyone who sympathizes with the Patriots, and is a member of their online site, moves to the formerly known North America. Everyone who sympathizes with the Freedom Fighters moves to the Atlantic coast of the former British Isles and so on. All people are searching for peace amidst global war. The movements of people amplify the war.

This is combined with different elements of the past that have survived the war and elements that have emerged out of the war. There is a juxtaposition of different eras in history living side-by-side. The old sailing ship, bartering and slavery, combined with high-tech online communities, tracking chips and space satellites. A new world is emerging. The declared factions that rule the old western world have introduced a new social structure and a financial system that undergirds this structure. The free faction world concentrated in Asia is trying to remain free of these systems and structures.


*Seven years and five months later*
*Crossing the Pacific Ocean*

After several weeks at sea, she becomes at ease with the ocean. She no longer wonders if a one hundred and sixty-ton blue whale or a massive and eternal black hole is below them. She is able to sit on deck and look out at the starry night, a pastime that she has grown increasingly fond of since sailing in Latin America with the Plague, Atlas and Rocket. She often thinks of the Plague and Atlas, wondering where they went after the battle at Ciudad Juárez. She doesn't dare to think that one or both of them might not have survived the battle. With the passage of time, the battle seems more and more unreal. Like something terrible that she dreamt.

They sail in the baking sun. The water is statically still, with only small ruffles rolling quietly across the surface. Within less than an hour, the picture has entirely changed. The scenario starts with the captain calling everybody on deck. "No one can stay below deck. It is too dangerous, because if the ship goes down, you will be trapped below deck." He looks at Rocket, who is clearly concerned. "At least, if you are above deck, you can get into one of the lifeboats." He has no time to wrap his message in comforting words. He delivers the brutal truth swiftly before turning around and going about his next task of preparation.

Long ropes are extended and tightened across the deck. "One

separate rope per line!" he yells. The captain turns to them again. "You, hold tight onto the rope. Hold tight! Don't let go!" he insists. Within less than fifteen minutes, the first massive wave rolls across the deck, giving them a fiery warning of what is to come. She doesn't understand why the sun is still shining. It seems like a contradiction of the elements. Violent, tormenting seas and a brightly shining sun.

She looks at Rocket. "We hold tight, my love. Know that I love you with all of my heart. No matter what happens, I have always loved you, and I will always love you." She tries to give Rocket a smile of comfort but fails before the next wave hits.

Her knuckles and hands are white from the strain of holding tightly and the icy-cold water. She barely notices it before the next wave mounts in front of her. It grows and grows. She follows it with her eyes and head. She holds her breath in awe, fear and necessity as the wave breaks high above her, hitting her hard over the head as it tumbles down across the deck. It washes everything away from the deck. Everything and every person not holding tight is washed away in the wave. Each wave has singular, monumental force. Each wave calls for a unique response, carefully measured to match its force.

She tries to catch Rocket's eyes between the waves. She briefly puts her hand over Rocket's and rapidly removes it to prepare for the next breaking wave. A rope is loosened. She hears yelling and screams as people are washed overboard.

She loses count of time, but her exhaustion is unsurmountable by the time the water returns in an instant to its former static state. While bending over, they try to catch their breath. Rocket and she are white with salt. Their hair is coarse, and their eyes can barely stay open. The salt is in every crack of their skin and hair. The deck is emptied of all things. Only the ropes and those that survived are left.

Below deck, water is still streaming down from the ceiling. Their food is ruined, while a couple of the large jars of fresh water have fallen over. "This is a real problem," the captain says when he sees it. "We must ration our food and drinking from now on. We still have some way to go before we reach Bali."

"Will we make it?" Rocket asks, concerned.

"We will see," the captain responds. "Otherwise, we have to become selective. Better some strong people survive than everybody going mad or dying. That is the way nature wants it."

# The Homecoming

The Patriots had their satellite hacked. In that instant, millions of followers worldwide became homeless. Their chip ceased to track. Patriots' followers were suddenly free to wander outside their territory without encountering sudden death.

This incident gave rise to epic disruptions across the world. A wave of battles came in the wake of their fall, as competing factions tried to claim their territory and convert former Patriots to their faction instead. Additionally, many former Patriots were taken as slaves. However, this incident also offered opportunities. At least, that is what she had thought when she insisted that the Plague, Atlas, Rocket and herself continue their march up through South and Central America to cross what was formerly known as the U.S. border at Ciudad Juárez near the Rio Grande.

With hundreds of free faction followers, they camped by the dried-out riverbanks of Rio Grande before they were sure everybody was there, and they could proceed on their journey. At the time, she erroneously thought they could enter this region and woo former Patriots to join their free faction. She erroneously thought their group of free factioneers could grow to a massive faction. They would gain strength in numbers. Through this strength, they would be able to settle and live in peace. She was wrong. It all went wrong. They were confronted by the Liberators, who already had a stronghold in North America. Confrontation, battle and downright slaughter of thousands of people followed. They had trusted in her. Believed in her.

Followed her. Followed her to their deaths.

When she closes her eyes at night, vivid images of the slaughter pass before her eyes. Of all her suffering, this is the second greatest one. The greatest suffering was losing her daughter, Ranger, to the Freedom Fighters. However, losing her daughter was a very personal suffering. The slaughter brought suffering on monumental scale. So many innocent people lost their lives that day because she made a wrong decision. She was blinded by greed and ambition. After the battle, she retreated into herself. She had no more ambitions other than to live in peace as a free person. She had no other wants or wishes.

As she lies there in the darkness of her old, neglected house in Canggu, she wonders how her daughter, Ranger, is. She has known X most of her life, and at a very rational level, she knows he is strong and capable of caring for her daughter and his heir. "Yet, the task placed on Ranger's shoulders is monumental," she reasons. "Ranger is bound to have to fight to keep her place in that world. On the other hand, it is not as if the task of the journey to Bali was easy either," she concludes. Still, her reasoning does not remedy the deep, black void inside of her that was once filled with Ranger. She longs for Ranger, her voice and smell.

*Almost eight years later*
*Canggu, Bali*

Her house in Canggu was left intact, albeit it testifies to the passage of time. It is neglected. When they walk through the beautifully carved wooden gateway to the small courtyard with stone pathways twisting and winding their way to the different rooms, they weep with gratitude. "It is even more beautiful than I remembered," she says while grabbing and holding Rocket's hand in a tight grip. They stand there, side-by-side, holding hands while taking in the full beauty of the house and its garden.

"It is a sleeping beauty," Rocket says. "Its beauty has grown with time and neglect." The garden that was once carefully manicured has spilled over into a luscious opulence of flowers and scents. Hummingbirds, butterflies, bees and other insects have taken over the garden. The garden has devoured the house, as branches of flowers enter every crack and opening of the house. Without its occupants, the house surrendered to the garden in much the same way as civilization gave way to nature in the wake of war. The only real victor of war is nature.

In war, leaving people's abandoned possessions intact is for some an irresistible task. For others, it is a mark of deep respect and hope. When the Danish Jews were taken away to concentration camps, in some incidents, survivor Jews reencountered, upon their return, their homes were entirely intact. Even flowerpots had been tended to and the fridge was stocked with fresh milk. When they entered their homes after the indescribable atrocities they had experienced, it was as if time had stood still in their old lives. This says a lot about the Danes. It also says a lot about how the Danes experienced the Second World War. When the Germans rolled across the Danish border, the Danes immediately surrendered. The power imbalance provided no other viable path forward.

Small places are peaceful places, because they know that meddling with the big, powerful enemies only draws unwanted attention. Staying under the radar is the best survival strategy, while using skillful diplomacy and clever trade arrangements to stay friends with everybody ensures that some small places fare well through most global conflicts and wars.

Nevertheless, before the eruption of this Third World War,

the Danes encountered numerous scandals that fueled online communities and positioned the country for war. Danish authorities were caught selling citizens' health data, harvested at a national scale, to foreign companies; they were caught selling national energy resources to secure lucrative private business opportunities for individual politicians; they were caught sharing secret intel stemming from tapping critical telco wiring that crossed Danish territory with a foreign government; they hosted foreign military bases on Danish territory; the Danish prime minister shut down one of the largest export industries due to a personal dislike of the industry, to name but a few. Unsurprisingly, in the corruption cases, where the sitting government was the instigator, the cases were not pursued by the police and courts.

What was skillful diplomacy had a dark flipside steered by the greed and ambition of individual politicians. The naivete of the Danish populace was stark in the face of the corruption of Danish politicians. Not only corruption poisoned Danish society. Sheer incompetence of the politicians also played a crucial role in turning the population against the politicians and into the arms of online communities. Yet, for a long time, keeping the population in check was largely possible through state-censored and curated communication media. However, as Danes moved away from the state-censored and curated communication media to global streaming services, even Denmark started to feel the ground shake under its feet as the population divided along the global lines of different online communities.

Bali largely escaped this war of minds, that was once again centered on the western powers. Unlike in Denmark, the Balinese people had never put much faith in their politicians. Thus, the Balinese people had cultivated a politician-proof resilient society.

They had created a society that operated without or rather despite the meddling of the politicians. This meant that the online communities gained less momentum in Bali. The online communities did not, as they had in Denmark, offer a tantalizing alternative universe of so-called free thinking and speaking. As the Balinese people knew deep inside what they were thinking, truly thinking, of the politicians and ruling class, they did not become disappointed by their corruption and incompetence. Additionally, the Balinese people were less drawn to the escapism of the online world. They were better able to live in the present. They lived in the here and now.

*Eight years and five months later*
*Canggu, Bali*

They go to the marketplace that day. It is early. The bright sun is only just ascending. She loves the early mornings. They hold the promise of the day. The whole day is ahead of you. You can decide what to do with it. The sun foreshadows the intense heat that it would shed later that day. As heat spreads, people are transcended into a haze of relaxation. This state of relaxation infiltrates people's minds. They become complacent, easygoing and friendly. In this way, the sun defines their culture. It is a culture of peace and relaxation.

"Look, mother!" Rocket yells. People all around them scream. Like they have been hit by invisible stray bullets, random people around them collapse to their death.

"What is going on!" she screams. Everybody starts running in all directions. Intense panic festers in every bone of her body. She wants to freeze, but she musters all her willpower to grab her daughter's hand and run. "We must get away from the marketplace! There's a sniper on the roof!" The collective fear activates animal instincts of fleeing, as everybody seeks safety.

Once out of the marketplace, they feel safe to stop and catch their breath. "Oh my God!" They look at each other with desperation in their eyes. Even outside the gates of the marketplace, certain people are collapsing to their deaths. "What is going on?" she asks in a high-pitched voice. People have stopped running. They are just standing still while holding their hands before their eyes and crying.

"What is this?" Rocket exclaims. Nobody knows. Nobody answers. People just shake their heads in resignation of the inexplicable.

They feel exhausted as they walk through the gateway of their front garden. "Are we safe anywhere?" Rocket asks, sobbing.

"I don't know. I don't understand," she says while dragging her body over the threshold of the gateway. They both go to their rooms. Before they know it, they are in deep sleep, fleeing from the horrors of reality into the world of dreams. It is as if their subconsciousness takes over to protect them from themselves. They are transcended into a comalike sleep, where their subconsciousness wrestles in peace with what they have experienced. The subconsciousness is stronger and more powerful than our consciousness. After all, the consciousness is ruled by mere mortals, whereas the subconsciousness is ruled by what lies beyond our consciousness. Our subconsciousness is the gateway to the other world. A wiser world. It calls on our loved ones that are dead and the angels that protect us. They all visit us in our dreams.

She hears a voice calling her name. It is calling her name somewhere in the distance far away. She is trying to wake up.

She is trying to regain consciousness. Suddenly, she opens her eyes and sees Birka, an elderly woman, who helps them with house chores, standing above her. She sits right up in her bed. "What time is it?" she says, confused.

"It is four in the afternoon," the woman says. Birka is a kind woman. She has become an irreplaceable helper in their household. She so appreciates Birka's company. They often sit, drink tea and talk for hours. Birka also comes from the northern part of Europe. She fled with her son. Unlike her, Birka lost everything in the war, except her most precious possession: her son. She did not have cryptocurrency or any other assets of value that she could bring with her into this world. She has the demeanor of a woman of considerable social standing. She is well educated and well informed.

"What happened?" she says while reaching her hand out into the air, fumbling to catch Birka's hand.

Birka takes her hand calmly and says, "It seems that somehow the Patriots' satellite was reactivated. They must have been working on it ever since it broke down many months ago." She looks down. A tear rolls down her cheek. Birka continues, "All the Patriots outside their territory were killed. The chip released the venom."

"Thousands of Patriots must have died!" Rocket intervenes as she approaches them. "This is insane!"

As time will show, Bali is sheltered from the war, except for intermittent incidents, such as this one. Most of these incidents are spillover effects of a war being fought elsewhere between declared factions. There is no direct face-to-face, fist-to-fist war in Bali.

*Eight years and five months later*
*Isle of Wight*

Ranger's life is lived in the hotbed of fighting, in what was formerly known as Europe. Yet, Ranger's life is also lived in substantial luxury. "I don't need all these things!" she complains to X.

"Yes, you do, because these status symbols position you as a person of great importance and power," X says and pauses before he continues, "I don't care much for these clothes, staff, houses and ships either, even though I like our house! It is ridiculous that all this is only there to arouse awe and respect from the people around us."

"The whole thing is staged!" Ranger responds with a sharp voice. She feels like a rebellious teenager, which is reinforced by X's overbearing treatment of her. "I would trade the luxury any day for a life lived with real people. I have no friends. I miss my old life." She slams the door as she leaves the room. She goes back to her room. Her yearning for her mother and sister is unbearable. What they had was so close. They were inseparable. She blames X for taking her mother and sister away from her.

When she comes out of her room again, she looks for Artemis, X's wife. Artemis is kind and compassionate. She can listen to Ranger for hours. The trouble is that Artemis does not have many opinions herself. At least, she does not share her views with Ranger. In fact, Artemis does have her own views, but her manipulations are so subtle that Ranger doesn't notice them. She thinks that Artemis is just there, with all her kindness and compassion. Listening. Ranger thinks her rather useless but seeks her, nevertheless, when she needs to unload her burden. She also knows that Artemis does not report on her to X and has her best interests at heart. Ranger is the daughter that Artemis always wanted. She is the future leader that X always wanted.

"I think we need to bring Ranger out of the house more. She

needs to see the world that she will one day navigate and reign in. It is not enough for her to know this island and its people," Artemis tells her husband when they meet that evening after dinner. "We need to show Ranger to the world, cementing her as a future leader. We need to demonstrate that she can continue in your footsteps." Artemis knows exactly how to spin her husband to her will. "She also needs to find a husband. We need to secure the bloodline."

X looks up at her "I was hoping she would find someone herself, fall in love and start a family."

"So was I." Artemis looks him in the eyes. "But she never leaves the house, the village or the island. You need to bring her along on some of your trips. If she never meets any peers, how will she ever meet someone?" Artemis' logic is reasonable and convincing.

"You know that she is choosy. Otherwise, she would have found someone already," X replies. She tilts her head in a disarming way. X continues, "I am scared something will happen to her." He looks down. "I mean, some of these meetings can go both ways. I could get killed. I told you… We are not even safe amongst our own. Everybody wants more power."

Artemis looks firmly at him. "Don't give me that! You also want more power. Ranger needs to learn the game if she is going to survive in this world. You need to teach her. How else will she learn?"

He nods in recognition. "You are right. I am just being overly protective of her." He pauses to think of the four children he lost to the war. "I will bring her along to the celebratory dinner next month in the House of Slora. You will also come. It will be a good opportunity for her to meet the leaders, their advisers and closest allies in a secure environment."

Artemis lights up. "That's the spirit! What can possibly go wrong at such a joyous event?"

The House of Slora rules on the mainland and along the coast, toward what was formerly known as France. They have an impressive fleet of twenty-four ships. Most recently, they have started to collect tax from the ships passing through the strait formerly known as the Channel. However, the other side of the strait is dominated by Prosperity, which also reigns in the northeastern part of the mainland.

The Freedom Fighters are squeezed on both sides from Prosperity. Nevertheless, the Freedom Fighters are saved by the fact that most declared factions, including Prosperity, are still finding their footing. In the interim, they are disorganized and distracted by internal power wrestling. The Freedom Fighters also have internal power struggles. With age, X is somewhat resigned to the power struggles. Since securing the future of his reign with Ranger, he has grown tired and content with the Isle of Wight, which presents a natural fortress. It also presents a bounty of riches, primarily from the sea. Almost all of his peers acknowledge his leadership of the Isle of Wight. He is left uncontested, as long as he does not pursue more land and power for himself on the mainland.

The House of Slora is his closest ally. However, some friction has recently emerged, as their leader, Abram, wants X to dedicate two large ships to his toll tax operation in the strait. "But you know, you will eventually go into combat with Prosperity over the right to collect taxes! Once they get sorted internally, they will look out toward their nearest vicinity to see how they can cement their power and conquer more land and wealth. It is just a matter of time before they come after you." X explains to Abram with great animation.

Abram smiles calmly. "No loss, no gain. I have to use this window of opportunity to accumulate more wealth and power in order to withstand their future attacks."

"I only have six ships in total," X replies. "If I lose two in combat, I cannot even protect my current position against the most prominent merchants on the Isle of Wight. Right now, the merchants are kept in check through the power balance, but if my power diminishes, they could decide to take advantage of my weak position. The merchants have more wealth, but my military power and prowess are superior to any of theirs." X catches his breath before continuing. "I am more interested in securing my power on the Isle of Wight for Ranger than investing in an adventure in the strait that may or may not render anything and might very well go horribly wrong."

The Isle of Wight is farther away from the strait, making territorial expansion to the strait impossible for X. However, Abram can accumulate both wealth and territory through this endeavor. He is also younger and more audacious, and he has a larger family, whose future position he is determined to secure. Abram assures X he will be amply rewarded by receiving a percentage of the taxes collected.

"How will I ever know if Abram tells me precisely how much he collects in taxes?" X complains to Artemis. "He can just as well lie. It is impossible for me to verify how much Abram has collected. We can easily fall out over this insane idea." Artemis is more inclined than X to accept Abram's offer. The conversation between X, Abram and their advisers continues. Yet, X hopes Abram will find the support he is looking for elsewhere.

"He who lives quietly, lives well," X tells Ranger. Ranger is a careful and highly perceptive listener. She has learned a lot about the world around her just by listening in on conversations at dinner and meetings held in their house. Abram visited them on two occasions to discuss the toll tax operation. Nevertheless, life in the house and on the island bores her. Her boredom makes her restless and sometimes reckless. In this way, Ranger takes after her mother, who was also restless and impatient in her younger days.

They decide to break the news of Ranger's coming out to her at dinner the following day. "We would like you to join us for the celebrations at the House of Slora next month," Artemis says, beaming like a sun. "Their son is getting married, and we are all invited to the celebrations." Artemis ponders. "Do you need a new dress?" she asks.

Without answering, Ranger exclaims, "This is great news! Thank you. Thank you for bringing me!"

In the subsequent weeks, X introduces Ranger to the toll tax dilemma. "It is important that you understand my position. Our position. We are not able to accept this offer. The potential losses outweigh the gains. If we lose two large ships, which I think is entirely possible, we will be unable to defend the island. Our position on the island will be threatened. Right now, with six ships we can defend the island. And if we lose ships and power, the merchants may rebel. One or more of the most prominent merchants will challenge me. Challenge us. The threats you meet from within are always the most dangerous threats. Civil war is always more dangerous than other wars that can be fought on another territory, away from home. Civil wars are also more poisonous. They poison the common well."

X uses every opportunity to deliver important lessons to Ranger. He continues, "After all, Abram will lead the battle, and he will probably send my ships into battle first rather than risk his own, if and when it comes to battle against Prosperity."

"What if it doesn't come to that?" she asks.

"That is inconceivable," X says in a loud voice. "Do you think Prosperity is just going to sit and watch while we collect taxes in what is indisputably also their marine territory?"

Ranger walks away in deep thought. In fact, it is this type of preoccupation that keeps Ranger out of trouble. She needs to be intellectually challenged with a worthy cause to stay dedicated and focused. Frivolity and a senseless waste of time and capacity make her lose focus and concentration.

While people around her seem to be more concerned about her dress and jewelry, she is trying to think about how to accommodate Abram's wishes while avoiding outright war with Prosperity. As always, she shares her reflections with Artemis. "Why can we not invite Prosperity to the negotiation table?" Ranger proposes to both X and Artemis one evening over dinner.

*Nine years later*
*Canggu, Bali*

Her mother's health is deteriorating. Sometimes, when her mother wakes up in the morning, she feels that she can hardly move. All the joints and bones in her body are aching. Years of wandering and strenuous travel have left deep marks on and in her body. She seeks a woman, Eirny, in the village, who is renowned for her healing hands. Before the war, Eirny attained her education from the Phenkhae Thai Massage School in Bangkok, Thailand, a state-accredited massage school focusing on healing injuries. She wonders if the school still exists.

"You have to make the mind the master of your body," Eirny says. Her eyes water, thinking of everything she has been through that has brought her to where she is today. "You are strong. You

138

can do this," Eirny insists. After several months of consistent pain in her left shoulder and arm, she is finally surrendering to Eirny. She has the utmost respect for people who perfect their craft.

In fact, it is when Eirny says, "You are strong. You can do this," that she starts to cry. All her life, people have told her how strong she is.

"Yes, that is true, but sometimes, just sometimes, it would be nice not to have to be so strong," she thinks as a tear rolls down her cheek. In that instant, she feels relief, like a heavy weight being lifted off her shoulders, as Eirny's skillful hands touch her body.

"Your pain is not in your back. Your neck and shoulders are just compensating for a pain located in the front of your left shoulder. I must do stretching exercises to remove that pain. The pain comes from an injury stemming from the battle at Ciudad Juárez. It will be painful to cure it. This is why you have to make your mind the master of your body. Your mind must decide to endure the pain that I inflict on you to cure you." Eirny's English language knowledge is modest. To make sure that she is well understood, she speaks in short and simple sentences that sound like commands. She obliges.

She bottled up the anger and resentment of losing Ranger. The bottled-up feelings are now located at the front of her left shoulder. Now that she can relax her mind and body, the pain has flared up and calls for her immediate attention. When Eirny pulls her arm in different directions, an excruciating pain travels to her fingertips and toes. "It is good you came here," she says, "I can help you."

"Mind over body," she thinks. "At what point do we let our feelings besiege our being, our mind and body?" We cannot just live in our feelings the whole time. Sometimes, our feelings are perfectly rational, but sometimes they are really just useless. Resigning to the power of negative feelings will eventually drive you over the edge. Anxiety, depression, resentment, jealousy and greed are all feelings that should be respected, addressed, dealt with and shut down. "You have to be able to see yourself from the outside. You have to be able to ask yourself, 'Is this feeling really helpful? Is this who I am? Or should I rather get in front of this feeling and shut it down before it gets the better of me?'" she reasons.

Before the war, the western world was riddled with feelings and people searching for feelings through all kinds of external stimulation. Drugs, medicine, food, sports, healing and so on were all examples of how to experience feelings in what was sometimes a numb, boring human existence. The feeling "I am feeling sad, but I don't know why" dominated the affluent western world and was potentially also a trigger to the war. If someone, after thorough searching, does not know the root cause of their sadness, anxiety or depression, it is probably because there is no reason. If, on the other hand, someone is sad, anxious or depressed because they face a difficult challenge, there may be a good reason indeed. If there is a real reason for a certain negative feeling, one must propel into action to change the negative feeling into constructive action. Overanalyzing sadness, anxiety and depression without doing anything about them was the root cause of many of the ills in the western world before the war. Negative feelings should be addressed, tackled and shut down. They should not be nurtured and allowed to grow out of proportion.

As she lay there on Eirny's mattress, she remembers Ranger saying, with excitement in her voice, "Having a diagnosis is so interesting. We have lots of kids in my class with a diagnosis, and they are so different." Her young mind failed to recognize that if lots of people have something, it is hardly different or unique.

"Maybe not having a physical illness or mental diagnosis will become a rarity in the affluent western world one day," she thought to herself in a life lived before the outbreak of the war.

Having lived most of her adult life abroad, she knew that in other parts of the world the need to simply survive keeps mind and body busy. "We do not have time for first-world problems," her Argentinian boyfriend had told her when she had asked why nobody had a diagnosis in Argentina. They drove across the old steel bridge taking them to Bernal in the southern part of Buenos Aires, where his parents lived. They went there every Sunday for family lunch, and she absolutely loved it. She loved his parents and sister.

In retrospect, she thought she might have stayed with him a bit longer just to revel in the wonderful Sunday family lunches a bit longer. She was totally aware that her first marriage and this relationship were emblematic of her searching for a family or something that resembled the closeness and love that you can only find in a family, albeit not all families enjoy such closeness and love. He was paying every month toward his parents' upkeep and for the education of his sister. That was what you did in those parts of the world. You lifted yourself and your family out of poverty. "That keeps you busy and gives you a cause worth fighting for," he had said resolutely.

In this way, her Argentinean boyfriend explained that Argentineans are busy surviving. Too busy surviving to concern themselves with overanalyzing sadness, anxiety and depression. Overanalyzing negative feelings was the prerogative of people in the affluent western world, he concluded. "Maybe if people make more of an effort with life, they will not get bored and search for trouble," she had wondered as they continued their conversation and journey across the steel bridge. "It is not just about ambitions. It also about living and experiencing new things. It is about living interesting lives," she had said.

"The monkey will move with you," her mother had said. "You cannot flee from the monkey. It is sitting on your shoulder." This was her mother's way of urging her to stop moving around the world and start looking within for whatever it was she was fleeing from on her travels.

Life is about balance. The balance between recognizing the feelings that are real and rational and that need addressing and tackling for us to become whole and sane human beings, and the feelings that are idle and useless and will only cause unhappiness and destruction if we pursue them.

Life is about balance. The balance between living responsible lives and living the time of one's life. It is a balance between under- and over-stimulation. Under-stimulation, or boredom, makes us do stupid things, such as taking drugs or endlessly pursuing a negative feeling that should not live in your mind and body to start with. Over-stimulation, or restlessness, will take us over the edge and make it impossible for us to lead a responsible and meaningful life.

Until she had children, her life tended to be over-stimulated. Whenever her life seemed to become stale, she would change, move, pack up and leave. This is why she had lived in so many countries by the time she became a mother. When she had her daughters, she became overwhelmed with responsibility. In fact, it was not love at first sight. It was responsibility at first sight. She realized then that life is also about consistency. Waking up, going to work, going to the grocery shop, cooking, cleaning, bathing and starting all over again the next day. Persistently doing the same things over and over again, at least for a period, till she could change it again to something else. Twelve years passed till she could go away again on one of her aimless travels alone. She preferred to travel alone, as there were fewer distractions. Traveling alone sharpens the senses.

Ten years later<br>
Canggu, Bali

Even though she had lived in Bali for almost two years by now, her mind and body were still on high alert, waiting for the next disaster to happen. "What am I going to do?" she asks Eirny after a couple of treatments. "If I am unable to relax in my mind and body, the pain will never subside. I need to learn again how to relax."

Eirny looks at her in an inquisitory manner. Maybe she has never heard that question before. She can see that Eirny is thinking of how to respond. Then her face lights up and she says, "You need to chant. Many times a day, you repeat the same chant over and over again, 'From now on, everything will be good. From now on, everything will be good. From now on, everything will be good…'"

She chants every morning and every night. She also chants in between when she remembers. One morning, she feels, when she says the words, "From now on…" that she is moving forward in a fast pace. Nothing is pushing her from behind. Rather, she is just moving effortlessly forward in midair. When she gets to the latter part of the sentence, "… everything will be good," she is stationary. If she tries to force the feeling of moving forward in midair, it ceases. She keeps chanting to recover the movement.

143

Sometimes, she chants for hours before recovering it.

She closes her eyes as she chants. She feels how the moist air of Canggu penetrates her body with every inbreath of her chant. She becomes one with nature in a different way than she had ever experienced before in the Fence and Forest of Spades.

The "Fence" is her favorite place of all the places in the world. It is situated in the northern part of what was formerly known as Denmark. The only place that matches the Fence is the forest she wandered in at night during her childhood, the "Forest of Spades."

The Fence was evacuated of human settlement around the fifteenth century due to drifting sands. In 1724, it was decided that the drifting sands might be stopped by planting heavy vegetation that eventually became a wild forest. The forest borders the beach of the Baltic Ocean. She didn't go to the beach because the open expanse of the beach has never attracted her.

In the "Fence," as in all old forests untouched by human hands for centuries, there are beautiful spiritual creatures that wash your soul with positive energy. These creatures are in the air. They stroke your cheek if you let them. They are beautiful and only hold good. Eternal good. They meet every person with good and wash every soul with positive energy. They only live in the forest.

There are also devious and sometimes evil trolls nestling around the forest bed. Pine forests are ideal for trolls because the evergreens provide a place to hide all year. They love moss because it is soft and keeps them warm in the winter. In the Fence, there is plenty of pine and moss. If you fear the trolls, they will come out and tease you. Because the trolls are borderline evil, they do not appreciate where to draw the line between teasing and downright dangerous evil. Therefore, you should not walk into the forest fearing the trolls. That only attracts their attention. To be on the safe side, it is probably best not to speak their names in the forest. There are low wetlands with dead trees and swamps in the Fence. Here, the psychic woman reigns. She does not always have good intentions. She would steer clear of the wetlands, maybe because the wetlands did not offer solid ground below her feet. Maybe because she feared the psychic woman.

Albeit all creatures of the forest are her friends, they all recognize her as one of theirs. She is totally safe in the forest. She can call on the beautiful, good creatures, the trolls and the psychic woman. She is not scared of any one of them. She is their equal.

*Twenty years earlier*
*South of France*

"You have to be better connected with your intuition," her friend told her. She knew this to be true already. She could ascribe most of her big mistakes in life to not listening to her intuition. The problem was not to listen to her intuition. The problem was doing as her intuition told her to.

She recalls a particular situation from her old life. Her husband had gone into town to meet some friends. She was alone with the girls in the house when intruders entered. "I knew these people were going to steal whatever they could. I also knew that if I got up and started walking around, I would encounter them, and things would go horribly wrong. I was lying there on the couch, thinking that they must have followed me from town to the house," she tells her friend. They took all her jewelry. At the time, she had quite a bit. "I knew exactly when they were in the house and that they were taking my jewelry. Yet, I did not call the police till after. In part, because I thought it was too weird," She looks up, "What was I going to say? 'I feel that someone is watching me and will break into the house and steal all my jewelry.'" She opens her arms as if to show how strange it would have been to call the police on a hunch. An intuition. "This was a scary incident. My focus was on letting them get away with my jewelry to save myself and my girls."

The real lesson of this incident – she has since recalled time and time again – was that the incident led to her intuition telling her that she should not move to France with her girls. She should stay away. Far away. Yet, her rational thinking told her that she needed to make an effort to rekindle her ailing marriage. The best way to do this was to move to France with the girls to be with her husband. Nevertheless, the minute she landed in the airport in France, she knew something was horribly wrong. "Had I just listened to my intuition and what the universe was trying to tell me loud and clear…" She sighs. She recognizes that she could intuitively feel what path to choose. The challenge was to do as her intuition told her. Her mind was constantly battling between her intuition and rationality.

Eleven years earlier<br>Denmark

The following day, she gets up early to go for a walk in the forest. Perhaps because of her early rise, she becomes overwhelmed with fatigue during the day. When she comes home, Rocket asks her if she can have the living room to herself. She is assigned her own room, which serves both as her bedroom and private parlor. As she sits down on the bed, her eyes start to give in to the fatigue. She falls into the rare and wonderful sleep that you can only get when you sleep in the middle of the day and in bright daylight. Daytime sleeping is like stealing hours from the day. In her dreams, she visits an old recurring dream, where she is in Bali buying her house. Her intuition is telling her she is going to spend longer periods of time in Bali. It seems totally natural. Almost matter-of-fact. Of course she will live in Bali. Her intuition tells her that this will happen, and she will find a way of making it happen. When she went to Bali before the war and purchased the house, it was an intuitive premonition of what would come. Bali is her sanctuary.

The past strenuous years – during which she had lost everything and was forced to keep on the move – left her feeling as if she was sliding headfirst down a spiral. She was spinning out of control. She was learning to let go of control and go with the flow. She was training herself to think positively, even when everything ahead of her promised to be frighteningly dark and completely unknown. She was Alice in Wonderland, falling into the rabbit hole. Like Alice in Wonderland, everything she encountered in this strange world around her seemed disproportionate. Things that should be small were big. Things that should be big were small. Things that were unimportant were important. Things that were important were unimportant. Everything was upside down. She was falling into the rabbit hole. The only things she had left to cling on to were her strong mental health and her intuition. "From now on, I will listen to my intuition. I will do as it tells me," she promises herself.

That night, she dreams that she is clawing her way up the inside of a brick chimney. Large bricks fall into the blackness below her while she is trying to open the ledge at the top of the chimney. On the other side of the ledge, a massive bright light is revealed. She is blinded by the light. Yet, she is determined to get out into the light. When she wakes up in the middle of the night, she lies in bed, still half in her dreams. She contemplates what the dream means. She chooses to interpret the dream as follows: after all their hardship, they have finally reached the end of their journey, where an all-consuming bright light awaits them. Bali is the bright light shining on them. For the first time in as long as she can remember, she smiles with happiness, relief and gratitude. A tear rolls down her cheek as she thinks, "Finally home. Finally, a place to settle in peace."

*Ten years and some months later*
*Canggu, Bali*

She wakes up as birds are singing loudly in the dead of night. There is an ear-deafening twittering. She walks out of her room to see what is happening. Rocket has also gotten out of bed. "What is going on?" Rocket says while looking at her mother and up into the sky. They can't see anything. Only the dark of night. Yet, they know something is wrong. Terribly wrong. The birds are sending them a warning.

An algorithm of one of the factions has ordered hundreds of drones to collect and categorize data on each individual faction member living in Bali. The algorithm calculates the most appropriate response to each person, including the release of the venom of the chip in every escaped declared factioneers, such as occurred several months earlier, when the Patriots' satellite was repaired and reactivated. Once the Patriots' satellite was up and running, the algorithm woke, and these drones were activated. The drones are the army of the algorithm. A parallel army to that of the humans. But whereas humans fight for their lives, the drones have an advantage over humans: they do not mind taking unnecessary risks that lead them straight into destruction and death. Precisely because of the drones' lack of fear, they are superior to human beings in combat. This is a fight between nature (represented by the birds) and technology (represented by the drones). Humans are stuck in limbo somewhere in between.

The drones are unlikely to harm her, Rocket and the rest of the free faction community she belongs to. Only if a declared faction wants to expand its territory will the drones attack and kill the people of the original settlement. Free factioneers living in large but isolated communities, such as the one in Bali, are an unlikely target of such territorial expansion. The fact that the community in Bali is relatively large with natural borders of an island make it an improbable target of the declared factions' ambition of expansion. Bali is a natural fortress for a relatively large and thriving population of free factioneers. On the other hand, Bali hosts important trade ports, such as Padang, that draw inauspicious attention from the declared faction leaders. Yet, its trading opportunities also help solidify and expand the wealth of the declared faction leaders by offering a neutral place, where merchants of different declared factions can exchange their goods and knowledge in a peaceful manner. Thus, reining in and taming Bali would kill off the declared faction leaders' opportunities to access goods and knowledge from different parts and factions of the world.

After more than a decade of war rolling back and forth across continents of the world, the global population has been reduced by more than half. In its place, nature has taken over. There is a new abundance of nature and animals. Humans, nature and animals live in harmony in places like Bali, where the human existence resembles that of the hunter–gather society some four thousand years ago before we started cultivating and exploiting the earth for farming. In Bali, people hunt and collect only the food they can eat. Its people are not on an eternal quest for growth and expansion. They are content with what they have, and they are willing to share with those who do not have. The land is owned by nobody. It belongs to nature. Its bounty renders the human existence on earth.

Yet in other places, such as what was formerly known as Europe, where Ranger now lives, declared factions have transitioned to farming. In this context, territory is critical. The more territory a person, family and faction possess, the greater the farming opportunities and wealth they possess. Before long, the declared factions are back on the eternal growth inertia from the old world, where the more land you possess, the more labor you need to cultivate the land. The more labor you have, the more land you need to feed the laborers. Population expansion leads to growth expansion. Out of the war, once humans take their eyes off the immediate emergent fighting, they focus on a new "old" target: growth. With growth comes greed, expansion and ambition. People will kill for land and labor.

Labor to farm the land becomes an important currency, making slavery widespread. In fact, there is a greater risk that she and others in her community will be taken as slaves than that their land will be taken over by one of the declared factions. In these declared faction societies, dormant systems and structures from the old world are awoken and reintroduced, such as slavery, day-laborers, taxes, social hierarchies, status symbols and so on. Art loses its beauty as it is transformed into the hard currency of the status symbol.

In this way, the global map is defined and reshaped into pockets of free factioneers who are searching for communities where everybody has equal rights, and food is largely shared to large territories of declared factions that are farming communities with hierarchies, hard labor, systems and structures.

Even now, a decade after the debilitating global migration, all humans remain on a journey. While people of the free factions in the hunting communities look for opportunities for growth within themselves, people of the declared factions in the farming communities look for opportunities for growth in the physical world.



During the last year, her mother's health and fighting spirit have deteriorated radically. Rocket is deeply concerned. Frown lines between her eyes are now a permanent feature on her face. She wants to get the word of their mother's deterioration to Ranger but doesn't know how to get in touch with her. She doesn't want to share her concern or her wish to contact Ranger with her mother, as her mother would realize that her concern and search for Ranger means Rocket is seriously concerned for her. Rocket doesn't want to worry her mother unnecessarily. In fact, her mother's poor health has become the elephant in the room. They both know that her mother's days are numbered, but none of them dare to voice their concern. Words would make it real. Once, it is said, it cannot be unsaid. Once it is said, it cannot be undone.

She decides to ask Birka if she knows how to get word to Ranger of her mother's poor health. "Maybe you know of some Freedom Fighters that are here in Bali on an errand? Some travelers?" She looks at Birka with curiosity. "You know, sometimes declared factioneers come here to trade."

"Does your mother know that you are reaching out to

Ranger? Will she approve of that?" Birka asks sharply.

Rocket explains that of course her mother will not want to worry any of her daughters, but she knows that Ranger will want to see her mother before it is too late. "I am in such a dilemma. If I tell my mother I am concerned and believe that Ranger should at least be offered the chance to come here to say goodbye to her, then I speak the unspeakable. The inevitable becomes evitable. It seems that mother and I have a pact not to speak of her deterioration. I want to respect that, but I also need to face the reality of the situation." Rocket's eyes start watering.

Birka nods. She too feels pressing tears. "I don't know of any Freedom Fighters here in Bali. I am not that well connected in this matter. But you can try Skipper, a gathering place for sailors and merchants in Padang along the coastline of Bai Lanka."

"Thank you," Rocket whispers and turns around. None of them can say anything more without crying.

The port of Padang is in the natural bay. She has never seen so many ships packed into such a small space. Along the harbor promenade, she stumbles across Skipper. She enters the place, ornamented with beautifully colorful wooden carvings along the paneled walls. She looks around the room to orient herself and sits down at a long table, where several men are seated. "Do you know how I can get a message delivered to someone in Europe? To someone in the Freedom Fighters?" She looks at them. They shake their heads, declining, and continue their conversation while ignoring her. "Do you know who can help me? Can you direct me toward sailors or merchants going to Europe?" No one answers.

During the chaos of war, many advances for gender equality eroded. Since then, patriarchal structures have been reintroduced in the declared factions together with all the other old social structures they have reinstated. In the free faction world, equality between the sexes remains.

She stays in Skipper for a while, hoping someone will approach her with an answer. Before long, she decides her endeavor is pointless. She gets up and looks around the room one last time before making her exit. "Thank you for nothing!" she thinks to herself as she walks back out into the bright sunshine.

The marketplace in Padang is known for its richness of spices, fruits and vegetables. The place heightens the senses. There is a myriad of people from all walks of life politely pushing past each other. People come from all over the world to Padang to trade. It is a meeting place of people of diverse factions, beliefs and cultures. Traders yell out names of produce that she does not recognize. She strolls around the market, looking for ingredients for a special dinner she will prepare for her mother. Her travel should not be entirely wasted, she reasons. She feels her mother needs to eat better to strengthen her health. Suddenly, a voice right next to her talks directly into her ear. "I can probably help you." He leans forward but retreats when he realizes she gets a shock. Henceforth, he tries to keep a respectful distance.

"Sorry, but what are you referring to? Who are you?" she says, bewildered.

"I may be able to help you deliver a message to the Freedom Fighters in Europe."

His name is Mr. Twinklestar. He has dark hair and eyes and fair skin. He is average of height and build. In many ways, he looks insignificant, but his charm disarms her as he says, "Can I invite you to a small teahouse around the corner, where we can discuss your matter of business in peace and quiet?" She looks wide-eyed at him. He reassures her, "I don't want to intrude on you. I just overheard your request in the bar and realized that no one seemed willing to help you. I can help you." He waves his hand in the direction of the teahouse. She follows with caution, mystified.

The teahouse has beautiful multi-colored tiles on the floors and walls, and large silk cushions on low, broad chairs. From the ceiling, soft dusty-colored tissue paper hangs. The warm air is penetrated by the scent of spicy tea. She feels nervous, but she doesn't understand why. They order tea, and he orders some assorted small Arabic cakes, "In case she is hungry." Mr. Twinklestar explains that he is a merchant of spices, tea and rice. He represents a series of high net worth clients in Europe that are very demanding and rewarding. He smiles. While listening with fascination, she laughs at his anecdotes about his difficult clients. She senses a longing for traveling again. "We traveled for many years before settling here," she says with enthusiasm, "My mother and me. We live here now to be as far away from the war as possible and to live peacefully as free factioneers. Are you a free factioneer?"

"No, I am a Freedom Fighter. A proud Freedom Fighter," he says, smiling.

"My sister is a Freedom Fighter!" she bursts out spontaneously.

"Really?" He looks at her with curiosity.

"Yes, she is the daughter of X. You know… X, on the Isle of Wight."

"I know of him," he says, positively surprised. "How can your sister be the daughter of X?"

She blushes when she realizes that she has put herself and her sister in a compromising situation. "It is a long story. I will not bore you with that now. Maybe another time. Right now, I need to get a personal message to my sister on the Isle of Wight. Can you help me?"

"I think I can," he replies.

She looks at him in an inquisitive manner and continues, "We live in Canggu. Will you come and visit us, and I can explain it all?" she asks.

"There are some wholesale distributors and traders I must visit while I am here in Bali. I always visit them to hand sample my goods for my demanding clients and to place my orders for the next visit. I can come by your place on the way around the country, and we can discuss how to proceed."

"Good idea!" she says while getting up. "Then that is settled." They agree to meet in two days in her home in Canggu.

On the evening of Mr. Twinklestar's visit, Rocket and her mother decide to serve up some fine food for their distinguished guest. Rocket knows she must tell her mother the real reason why she has summoned Mr. Twinklestar. "Mother," she takes a deep breath in her runup to breaking her news, "I met Mr. Twinklestar in Padang, as I told you. We had a brief conversation, where he told me he is a Freedom Fighter. He knows of Ranger!" She widens her eyes and looks at her mother in a confirmative way.

Her mother is surprised. "Why do you talk about Ranger to strangers? You put both Ranger and us is a difficult, even dangerous, position."

"I know. But hear me out," Rocket says while making her case. "I decided he seemed trustworthy. I have never done this before. And I promise never to do it again." Rocket pauses. "In any event, he is coming here this evening, as you know, and we will learn more about Ranger. Maybe he can get in touch with Ranger? Don't you see? Maybe she can come here!"

Her mother looks away. She feels like saying, "Why on earth

would you want Ranger to come here? To make such a long journey?" but she decides to remain silent, because she doesn't want to hear Rocket's answer. They are both thinking of the elephant in the room: her imminent departure from this life.

Oftentimes when things are spoken, they lose their meaning. Like a painting forming in your mind that loses its beauty once it materializes as a painting. Oftentimes when things are spoken, they become real. Sometimes things are best left unspoken.

Mr. Twinklestar makes his entry in no subtle manner. He arrives with two servants and bearing plenty of gifts. Her mother is delighted. "Who is this man? And where did you meet him?"

Rocket stares at her mother. "I already told you! I met him in the marketplace in Padang."

Her mother shakes her head. "But I don't understand what you were doing there? It is so far away."

"I am grown up. I do not have to explain my whereabouts to you. Anyway, I told you, I went there to purchase produce for the wonderful dinner I prepared for you," she says softening her voice.

"Yes, yes," her mother says, "you are right. I should not be nosy."

Mr. Twinklestar has also brought gifts for her mother. Rocket wonders why he is so nice and generous. After all, her mother and she are just two spinsters living in Canggu. "Maybe he is trying to get close to Ranger," she says to Birka, who is helping out in the kitchen. "Surely, Ranger could become an important client of his, if she is not already!"

"Or maybe he has heard of your mother's great achievements?" Birka responds firmly. Rocket goes back into the dining room, no less enlightened. Mystery surrounds Mr. Twinklestar.

After dinner, Rocket walks with him to the gateway of their pleasant house through a small sacred garden with running water and plenty of white orchids and other flowers. The pathway is lit by candles. "I have written a message for Ranger," she says in a secretive tone of voice. "I really need you to get word to my sister of my mother's poor health." Her eyes water.

"Yes, yes… I realize she is not in good health," he says in a consoling manner while putting his arm around her shoulder. "She is a formidable woman. Her achievements are well known. She managed to create a massive following of free factioneers, many of whom have since settled here."

"Yes, but many of them died," she says, shaking her head. "Do you know that? That is why we do not talk much about what happened. I think my mother still regrets the battle at Ciudad Juárez. Of course, she could not have foreseen the battle. We still have not found some of our closest friends and traveling companions during those years."

"This war…" he says, also shaking his head, "There are no winners. Just losers."


Eleven years later<br>Bali


Over the next couple of years, Mr. Twinklestar grants Rocket a visit on a regular basis every time he is in Bali on business. "Are you sure it is not you he is interested in?" Rocket's friend asks her. "It seems peculiar he should visit you when he has no errand with you." Their relationship evolves into a deep friendship and later into a passionate, loving relationship. Yet, he is never willing or able to make any plans with her. She stops asking him when she will see him next time. She wonders if his aversion to

157

commitment has a deeper root cause.

"Are you married?" she intuitively asks one day as they are walking along the beach, holding hands and watching the sunset.

"Yes," he says to her great astonishment, "but I am in the process of leaving her." It is the oldest story in the world. Even in this new world, patriarchal structures persist. The context is new, but people largely remain the same.

Since the war, both marriages and divorces persist. Priests conduct marriages. Lawyers conduct divorces. The marriages and divorces are formalized and consolidated through public announcements on the online community.

Every time Rocket and Mr. Twinklestar meet, they argue about his lack of commitment to her and continued commitment to his wife, whom he reassures her he no longer loves. "Why can you not leave your wife? Why can we not live together here in Bali?" Her constant nagging and his ingenious avoidance of committing to her and their relationship take a toll on them, as arguments become more and more frequent.

From where she is standing, at a distance, it seems his whole family is in a conspiracy to retain unsurmountable mental and psychical illness thriving in the family. Eventually, persistent illness leads to the self-reinforcing need of one another. His daughter needs to be ill for the mother to set out on a quest to find a cure, which is impossible, as the daughter's illness is imagined. The father, Mr. Twinklestar, is the silent but reliable financial backer of the expensive endeavor. The older daughter is also ill, but she has since moved away. The wife threatens to commit suicide if he leaves her. Not because she loves him, but because she needs the theatre to go on. She needs him to play his part for her to play her part.

Playing their roles with bravos gives each of them a meaning of life. A sense of purpose. He almost never sees or engages with his daughters and wife. Only when they need something do they reach out to him, or when he apprehends that he is about to change the dynamics of the family by, for instance, divorcing. Then they all get involved and engaged to make sure he does not stray from the parameters of the role assigned to him.

He tells himself, and Rocket, that he is weighed down by the obligations to his ill family. This self-staged, self-sacrificing role suits him well. All the while, his focus is entirely directed toward the one thing in life that he is unquestionably highly successful at: his work. Albeit endlessly complaining about how busy he is, he thrives on his professional achievements. He escapes the reality of his dysfunctional family into his work, that flourishes because of the endless time, effort and energy he invests in this escapism. His desire to escape is strong.

No one can break away from this unspoken conspiracy, where everyone plays their part and a critical role. If one person breaks away, the whole thing falls apart. They would be forced to recognize that the whole thing is one big pointless theatre. They would have to confront the fact that maybe there is no illness. Maybe no one will commit suicide. Maybe they would each become happier by taking responsibility and living their own lives. After all, responsibility makes us grow and flourish. Nevertheless, if one person breaks away, the others would be forced to find a new purpose in life. Fearful of the realization that the theatre is all pointless and fearful of the unknown, they hold each other in an iron grip. No one is allowed to escape the theatre. He can never belong to Rocket.

In the early days of the relationship, they planted the seeds of an unhealthy pattern of her setting ultimatums and him making promises that he later breaks. He wants to keep the promises, but every time he tries to escape the theatre, his two grown-up children and wife start a new act of illness, suicide and misery. As early as three months into the relationship, he reassures her, "I will get divorced by summer." Summer passes. "I will get divorced by the end of the year." The year passes. "I will get divorced after my daughter's wedding… After my daughter's divorce." Their relationship becomes consumed by her ultimatums and his broken promises. Several years into the relationship, they are pretty much at the same place as they started. They meet up, have sex, conversations, wine and dine. No information. Minimum planning. No commitment. They are going in circles and never getting anywhere.

By the time she breaks up, because he does not break up but rather wishes to continue their relationship ad infinitum, stringing her along, she has given up on them ever becoming a couple. "Next time you have an extra-marital affair, make sure you tell the woman involved that you will never leave your wife." Rocket looks at him with stern sincerity. "I am not judging you. You can have extra-marital affairs, as you have had so many times before. All I am saying is that you owe it to the women involved to be honest and truthful with them rather than stringing them along with sweet nothings." He turns and walks away. He feels unjustly treated by her, which is ironic considering that he is the one staying married and lying to her. Rocket decides there is no point in engaging with him further.

*Twelve years later*
*Canggu, Bali*

Rocket has a far more urgent and important task to attend to. Her mother is not well. Every time Rocket thinks of losing her mother, she feels her throat closing in, like a rope being tightened around her neck. It gives her a deep unrest and pain in her chest. The thought of losing her mother makes her physically ill. Yet, there is no point in avoiding the facts of life. We will all die eventually.

Rocket enters her mother's room. It is a large room, with darkly painted wooden walls and hard-pressed earth on the ground. The air is cool inside. It smells of earth. There are no windows, but a lot of candles cast light all around her. Clothes are scattered around the room. Three people are sitting on low stools, one of whom is Birka. Their backs bend over. They look like small curled-up hedgehogs. The air is thick with sorrow. She walks up to her mother and stands next to her bed. Once holding her mother's hand, she forgets everyone else in the room. She holds her hand in a firm grip. "Don't leave me. Don't leave me. Don't leave me all alone in this world," she sobs. "There is still so much I need to tell you." She sits down on a stool next to the bed and curls up like a hedgehog.

After an indefinite time, she suddenly gets up. "I promise I will continue your life in me. I will live my life true to what you believe in and fought for. I will tell your story. I will never forget your ideas and thinking." After saying this, her throat loosens up. She can breathe for a while.

The day after, Rocket wakes up late, toward the early afternoon. She sits up and looks out into the day in bewilderment at her deep sleep and dreams. She feels guilty for sleeping a day away when her mother's days are numbered. She immediately goes to her mother's room, where Birka is still sitting, bent over. It looks like Birka hasn't moved an inch since the day before. She is too absorbed in her own sorrow to feel or show any gratitude to Birka and the other women sitting in wake by her mother.

This glorious day, her mother is sitting up straight in bed, eating soup. "It is so wonderful to see you so well," Rocket says and runs up next to her mother. For an instant, Rocket remembers that people who are dying have a momentary burst of life just before they die. Her mother insists on telling the story when her dead mother left.



Her mother pulls the curtains abruptly aside to reveal the large window. They are on the twenty-second floor of the hospital. The view is breathtaking. Normally, this view is almost depressing, overlooking large social housing complexes built in the 1970s, warehouses, truck parking lots and other industrial facilities. Today, the view is breathtaking. The landscape is covered in a thick layer of white snow that softens every sharp edge. The snow crystals reflect the intense winter sun. "This is worth living for!" she thinks as the curtains are pulled aside like in a theatre. The final act.

The mother tilts her head to look out of the window. She is standing with her back turned to her mother's bed, looking out at the scenery for a long while. "This is worth living for!" she says loudly to her mother and turns around. Her mother looks at her and smiles. She may have something worth living for, but she does not have the force or the will to go on.

She wonders if the Alzheimer's serves as a cover for her mother. An excuse for not having to confront the reality of the situation. An excuse for not having to say goodbye to her children and grandchildren. Her mother had always shied away from difficulty. Her mother did not need an excuse for not saying goodbye to her own mother, Rocket's grandmother, because, in this matter, Rocket's mother's denial was so immense that she would not even entertain the thought of her mother leaving her, little less discuss it with her mother or anyone else, for that sake. Alzheimer's created an invisible wall between the mother and the daughter. They couldn't really reach each other. Sometimes, she tried to look intensely into her mother's eyes to see if she could penetrate that wall. It didn't seem to work. Alzheimer keeps her mother in a childlike universe.

Every person entering Rocket's mother's realm during her mother's last weeks knew of her mother's imminent departure. Yet, no one spoke of it. She filled the room with intense wishful thinking and encouraging slogans. "You can make it!" "Come on, mum, you have so much worth living for!" She even pleaded, "Please, you cannot leave me!" This sentence haunted her for years to come. "How could I be so insensitive as to plead with my dying mother to stay, when that decision was not hers to make?" She hit herself in the head. "Why did I not spend the last time with my mother telling her how much she meant to me and how much I loved her?" She had done it all wrong. In those last weeks and days, she had only thought of herself. She had only thought of how she could claim and attain more of her mother for her. She was taking when she should have been giving.

They call in the middle of the night. She jumps up and answers the phone before she can think. "Hallo?"

"Your mother has just passed away." Her mother had specifically told the hospital nurses to tell her first.

"What?" She throws herself violently around in the bed while repeatedly yelling, "Why? Why? Why?" She is living a nightmare. The emotional distress and pain are excruciating.

"Is there someone we can call?" the concerned nurse at the

other end asks.

"No, there is no one!" No one was closer to her than her mother. She can't deal with anyone at this point.

Once the nurse hangs up, she goes back into deep sleep. It is almost against her will that she falls asleep. Like a force inside her that is not hers. After two hours, she wakes up quietly. She lays in bed, thinking of the reality that is slowly dawning on her. She will never see, touch, smell or kiss her wonderful and loving mother again.

She is calm as she walks into Ranger and Rocket's room. It is one at night. "Grandma is dead," she says while gently touching their shoulders to wake them. "We have to go to the hospital to say goodbye." Rocket and Ranger are eight at the time. They are confused, which soon turns into deep concern for their mother. They get up quietly, put on their clothes and walk solemnly out of the door.

Once in the car, she knows, it is dangerous to drive. She can't see out of her eyes for unstoppable tears. She clings to the wheel, weeping. Everything around her is swimming in tears. To make things worse, there is a thick layer of snow, which is impossible to navigate. Between the tears and the snow, she is driving into the white nothingness. On a couple of occasions, the car seems to be stuck in the high snow. Massive snow plows move around the empty streets at ridiculously high speed. They obviously feel they have the night and streets to themselves. She tries to collect herself and concentrate. She clings to the wheel while the tears run down her cheeks. She sobs.

"Why did you open the window?" she yells at the nurse when she walks into her mother's room. "You let out her soul before I could say goodbye." She sits down and cries unconsolably into her hands. Her head is aching from all the crying. After a while, she manages to collect herself. She turns to the nurse. "It is okay that you opened the window. If you don't let her out, she cannot travel to the other world. If she gets stuck here, she becomes a ghost." She knows this is true, but she says it aloud to erase the blame she initially placed on the nurse. They are on the same page.

That year, death is white. Everything is covered in bright white snow. It is beautiful, yet totally barren. She feels empty inside. The loss is unbearable. As weeks, months and years pass, she realizes that nothing in life means more than our close human relationships. These relationships bring love and life. The biggest loss in life is the loss of love and life. Nothing replaces that. All other things in life are replaceable. But nothing replaces the loss of love and life. Death is eternal. Death is white.

*Twelve years later*
*Canggu, Bali*

As she lies there in her deathbed, she realizes the universe is her friend and not her foe. Throughout her life, the universe threw challenges at her so that she might live to her full potential. While in the juggernaut, fending off challenges, one more impossible than the other, she was alarmed at what life had in store for her. Yet, now, toward the end of her life, she is grateful for each and every one of these challenges, as they revealed her proper path. Had she not encountered these challenges, she would not have been forced to change the course of her life. She would not have woken up every morning with a lack of purpose until her true purpose suddenly one day revealed itself. She learned to trust the universe and embrace her course of life with deep respect.

As she lies there in her deathbed, she recalls a time, many

years ago, when she cursed at the universe, telling it to leave her alone. Now, in hindsight, she recognizes the universe kept throwing challenges at her to make her course correct. She was not walking in the right direction. She was going astray. Today, her higher consciousness is an integral part of her being. It allows her to connect with the universe. Through her higher consciousness, she is in almost daily contact with her deceased mother. Soon, her daughters will embark on a similar journey to reach their higher consciousness, the realm of departed souls.

*Twelve years and a couple of weeks later*
*Canggu, Bali*

Rocket thought her mother's death ridiculed life. After all the extreme endurances that her mother had experienced, she died of mere old age in her sleep that night.

*Twelve years and a month later*
*Canggu, Bali*

About a week later, a hectic, loud knocking wakes her in the early night. She lives alone in the house now. Birka has left. She gets up and walks cautiously to the gateway on the other side of the garden. "Who is it?" she inquires.

There is a pause. "It is me! Ranger"

She almost faints with excitement. An instant compulsion rushes through her stomach as she opens the gate, opens her arms and embraces Ranger. The sisters both sob, hug and kiss. When she collects herself, she mutters, "Mother is dead. Mother is dead. Mother is dead." She has not said this before now. It was too painful to speak out loud till now, when she can share her grief with her sister. The only other person in the world who truly understands what she is going through. As she says it, she feels the pressing pain in her chest lifting. They both sob.

"I cannot forgive myself for coming here too late," Ranger says as they sit on the porch overlooking the garden. A full moon is shining. Its light reflects in the running water of the sacred garden. Its light illuminates the garden and house. It looks like a fairytale. They are living a fairytale as they sit together all night, talking about where they have been and what they have done all those years apart.

"You have to forgive yourself," Rocket says. "You remember that mother never forgave herself for not saying properly goodbye to her mother? You should not go through the rest of your life with the same burden, guilt and grief."

"Thank you for finding me. Thank you for the note," Ranger says repeatedly, almost as if she is chanting. "I came as quickly as I could." With different insertions of declared factions scattered across the world, a faction leader can always find home away from home. This enabled her safe journey.

"I am surprised X let you come," Rocket says in an inquiring manner.

"I did not need his permission," Ranger firmly replies. "He is dead." After a short pause, Ranger continues, "Artemis still lives, but she is old and has withdrawn from the world. I do like her, and I worried about leaving her behind, but I had to come. I had to come and say goodbye to mother." Her eyes well up. Rocket takes her hand. "Mother spoke of you every day. You never left us. You were always with us."

Ranger cries quietly as she says, "You never left my thoughts. I knew I had to find you again one day."

They both lie in Rocket's bed, holding each other. "I am no

longer alone," Rocket thinks before closing her eyes.

The next day, Rocket tells Ranger about the strenuous travel they undertook after leaving her on the Isle of Wight. "I think we must have traveled for at least a decade," she says.

"It is a miracle that mother was able to endure the hardship of the travel. Both the physical and mental hardship."

"First, we went to Buenos Aires, as the Plague insisted. We had a good life in a large warehouse, where at least a hundred free factioneers settled with us. But with time, we had to move on, both because the authorities were getting on mother's back and then the war caught up with us in Buenos Aires."

"I heard about that," Ranger says. "You know, before X died, he told me that mother and you moved the trackers with you, so that we always knew where you were. He told me that the last time the trackers were on, you were in Bali, so I knew I wanted to come here and look for you. This is where the trial stopped. This is where your journey stopped. But I had to wait till X was no longer alive. He didn't want me to visit you. I think he was always scared that he might lose me to you."

"Mother and I often talked about you visiting us once X was no longer here. We were both hopeful of seeing you again. It is such a terrible pity that mother never got to see you." They both pause to reflect.

Rocket continues, "We moved on from Buenos Aires to Cariló to see if the Plague still had some family there. He wanted to make sure he reconnected with his family before we left Argentina. Anyway, his family was nowhere to be found. Then, from there, we moved to Cusco, Lima, Quito, Buenaventura and finally we sailed to the Gulf of Mexico and continued by foot to Ciudad Juárez. Here, we were confronted with an army of the Liberators, who took mother and me hostage." Rocket catches her breath. Just recounting the travels is like running a marathon.

"What a crazy story," Ranger says.

"Yes! And you came to our rescue! You did!"

"That is true, but it must remain our secret. I bought your freedom behind X's back. In any event, X was very distracted during his last years, as he started writing his life story in the belief that he could shape the memory of his life in his favor. He wanted to make his life legacy eternal by writing it down. Such vanity!" Ranger smiles. "By the way, that Liberator's general who held you hostage, was an impossible man. He kept demanding a higher and higher ransom. I knew I had no choice but to buy your freedom." Ranger is still markedly upset about the situation. "Did you get the money I gave you?"

"Yes; with that money we were able to continue our journey to Bali. If you had not given us that money, our freedom would have been worth nothing. What is freedom with no money? Then we would have been free to starve. Most probably, someone would have taken us as slaves."

The days pass, and the sisters tell each other everything. They do not withhold any information, because they know they can fully trust each other. "Do you know what happened to the Plague and Atlas?" Rocket asks Ranger in a wild shot.

"Yes! The Plague came back to the Isle of Wight and looked me up. He is the one who told me that you were ambushed by the Liberators at Ciudad Juárez. He is the one who told me that you were taken hostage. That is why I was not surprised when the general's messenger looked me up in private. Normally, that would be a cause for suspicion and alarm. I have learned I can trust no one!"

"Oh, you know where the Plague is?" Rocket says, jumping up and down. "Is he safe?"

"He is safe and well. He is living in my complex on the Isle of Wight. He is old and a bit grumpy. He knows that mother was dying, but he himself was too old to make the journey. He wanted to, but I could not allow that. He would not have survived the sea journey across the Atlantic." Ranger continues, "I have been viewing the Plague almost as family and as my only link to you and mother."

"What happened to Atlas?" Rocket inquires.

"The Plague told me he died at the battle of Ciudad Juárez."

"How sad," Rocket says. "What a waste."

Still twelve years and a month later<br>Ubud, Bali

The following day is a glorious one. "I still have mother's ashes," Rocket says with hopeful eyes, like those of an excited puppy. "She wanted to be laid to rest in the forest. You know. That is where she felt at peace and at home. That is her final resting place."

"Thank you," Ranger whispers. "I am grateful that I can put mother to rest with you." They decide they will go the next day to the large forest in the middle of the island, near Ubud. Rocket asks Birka, who is now living with her son and his family, to help arrange some transportation for the day.

"Your mother would be grateful to know that Ranger is here. To know that you are not alone," Birka says.

As they sit in the small chariot, Rocket says, "You know the man who delivered the message to you?"

"Yes?"

"Well, I had a several years' long, long-distance relationship with him."

Ranger looks astonished. "But you know he is married?"

"How did you know?" Rocket looks at her.

"Of course!" Ranger says, "You do not have access to our online platform, where marriages and divorces are announced. We can just look up fellow factioneers' family status and relations." Ranger pauses before she continues, "I thought him quite cheeky and savvy myself. Out of curiosity, I decided to check him out online." Rocket remembers that Mr. Twinklestar is also a Freedom Fighter. "Were you sad to see the relationship break up?" Ranger asks her.

"Yes. I felt I had wasted some of the best years of my life to find myself suddenly all alone after we broke up and mother died. It would have been nice to have had his support and comfort me through this period of deep grief and loneliness. Of course, his leaving does not compare with mother's death, but it would have been nice to have had someone to share my life with at this stage." Rocket looks at Ranger. "Now I have you. That is all that matters."

"I don't know how long I can stay," Ranger says after a short while, "But you can come with me! I would love to have you come with me!"

"I don't know…" Rocket reflects. "I promised mother to live my life true to her. True to what mother believed in and fought for. Our community has evolved very differently from yours."

There is an unsubtle criticism of Ranger's life in that sentence. Ranger decides not to comment further. Instead, she says, "Think about it. It is an open offer."

They walk up the sloping side of the cliff to the top, from where the view over the forest is magnificent. A cool breeze catches them at the top. In the middle of the island, the weather is more temperate. They stop to take in the beauty of the scenery.

"What a wonderful place to live," Ranger says to Rocket. "And there is no war here? You have lived in peace all these years?"

"Yes, to a large extent. Nevertheless, we have had a couple of unsettling reminders of the war. Ragnarok is everywhere."

As they sit down to unpack the picnic basket packed by Birka, Rocket tells Ranger of the day at the marketplace when the Patriots' satellite was reactivated. "Did you have a similar experience in Europe when the Patriots' satellite was reactivated?"

"No, because homeless factioneers are only welcome if they become Freedom Fighters. Otherwise, they become slaves. If Patriots convert to the Freedom Fighters, we take out their Patriots chip and reinsert our own chip," Ranger explains.

"Ah, yes. You are right. Well, on this island, all kinds of people settle. But I guess most people are free factioneers." Rocket also tells her of the drones that came in the middle of the night, and how mother and she were woken by the birds that warned them.

Ranger talks about her past, and how the death of X was immediately followed by her taking over the reign of the Isle of Wight. "I did not feel up to the task," Ranger explains with earnest sincerity in her voice. "I felt like I was pushed into a role that I did not want. But I have since grown into the role. My most noticeable achievement happened right before I left. I negotiated a tax collection operation with both the House of Slora and Prosperity. If I had not been in the middle of these negotiations, I would have come here earlier, in time to see mother before she passed away."

She looks down and releases a tear. "In any event, I instigated and conducted large negotiations that have been in the works since long before X died. X and I had different views on the matter. He felt that we should decline the invitation to collaborate with the House of Slora. He rightly envisaged that collecting taxes in the strait would wake the rage of Prosperity. My suggestion was to get closer ties to both the House of Slora and Prosperity. Such a trinitarian unity cements each of our positions and prevents a flaring up of war between us in the future."

Ranger continues, "Together, we have forty-four ships. We block the passage of the strait. Yet, without my knowledge, they sank the first ships passing the strait just to show that they now rule in combined force and collect taxes. It was a way to spread horror and fear."

"Wow, you are really conducting grand politics," Rocket says, in awe of her sister. In this new world, women are commonly believed to possess greater diplomatic skills than men.

During their deliberations, it becomes clear that whereas Rocket is on the internal journey of living her life true to her mother and in deep faith of what her mother believed in and fought for, Ranger is on an external journey to cement power and accumulate wealth. East meets west. New world meets old world.

After hours of talking, they get up to throw the ashes of their beloved mother over the cliff and out on the forest below them. They each say a prayer to their mother. "Dear mother, I love you with all my heart. You will always live in my heart. I will hold you dear and protect you. I will live my life true to your being and your beliefs. I love you," Rocket says.

"Dear mother. Not a single day has passed without me thinking of you. I have felt your presence within me as a burning light of love. I love you forever," Ranger says. They both cry as they plant a magnolia tree where they stood when they released the ashes. This tree is their earthly connection with their mother.

They promise to always come back to the tree every autumn it blooms, on their mother's death day. A promise they both know will be impossible to keep. They turn around and walk back on the dense forest pathway that they came from. They comfort each other, embrace and hold hands.

THE END